IT'S NEVER TOO LATE

When Rebecca Summer is contracted to work as a temporary secretary for businessman Luca Barsetti on the Italian island of San Andrea, she thinks she can handle it — even though she was infatuated with him eight years ago at university. Much to her dismay, however, she finds that Luca's charms have not dimmed with time, and he appears to return her feelings. But she's now a confident, independent woman, far too sensible to fall head over heels for him again . . . isn't she?

Books by Wendy Kremer
in the Linford Romance Library:

REAP THE WHIRLWIND
AT THE END OF THE RAINBOW
WHERE THE BLUEBELLS GROW WILD
WHEN WORDS GET IN THE WAY
COTTAGE IN THE COUNTRY
WAITING FOR A STAR TO FALL
SWINGS AND ROUNDABOUTS
KNAVE OF DIAMONDS
SPADES AND HEARTS
TAKING STEPS
I'LL BE WAITING
HEARTS AND CRAFTS
THE HEART SHALL CHOOSE
THE HOUSE OF RODRIGUEZ
WILD FRANGIPANI
TRUE COLOURS
A SUMMER IN TUSCANY
LOST AND FOUND
TOO GOOD TO BE TRUE
UNEASY ALLIANCE
IN PERFECT HARMONY
THE INHERITANCE
DISCOVERING LOVE

WENDY KREMER

IT'S NEVER
TOO LATE

Complete and Unabridged

LINFORD
Leicester

First published in Great Britain in 2016

First Linford Edition
published 2017

A catalogue record for this book is available
from the British Library.

ISBN 978–1–4448–3472–7

Published by
F. A. Thorpe (Publishing)
Anstey, Leicestershire

Set by Words & Graphics Ltd.
Anstey, Leicestershire
Printed and bound in Great Britain by
T. J. International Ltd., Padstow, Cornwall

This book is printed on acid-free paper

1

Luca Barsetti leaned forward and picked up the secretarial agency's info folder from his desktop. He flipped it open, glanced at the top sheet, straightened, and then looked at the woman approaching his desk. Rebecca noticed that one of his hands was bandaged.

His dark eyes narrowed. A casual observer might think they were black, but Rebecca knew they were the colour of dark chocolate. She hoped that he'd recognise her immediately. His expression gave nothing away, so she automatically held out her hand. 'Good afternoon, Mr. Barsetti! I'm Rebecca Summer.'

He shook her hand briefly; his grip was warm and firm. He examined her appearance longer than necessary, noted she was barely as high as his shoulder, with a slender body and slim hips. Thick brown hair capped her head and brushed her shoulders. Her expression was interested and intelligent.

He gestured to one of the opposite chairs. She sat down, folded her legs neatly to the side. The afternoon sun was on the wane, but it was still pleasantly warm outside. The view from his office overlooked a park. She glanced at the greenery outside. It unconsciously helped her to relax, just a little.

He studied her face closely. Normally he had a good memory for faces and places, and he was almost sure he'd seen her somewhere before — but where?

'You know why I need your help?'

Rebecca was nervous, and she also felt a twinge of disappointment because he hadn't recognised her. She licked her lips; her throat felt dry. It was strange to face Luca again, after all this time.

'You want to write a non-fiction book about how to negotiate and optimise business dealings. You need a secretary for typing and researching.'

'Yes, that's it in a nutshell! I've wanted to write this book for some time, and already have some relevant information, but I've never had enough time to get it down on paper . . . until now. I mentioned it to a publisher I know; he likes the idea and wants to see a rough version in four to five weeks' time. Normally, I dictate into a machine and get someone in our central office to type it up, then correct it myself.' He lifted his bandaged hand for a second. 'But, as you see, at present I'm handicapped. And, as this book is a purely personal undertaking and nothing to do with the family business, I decided to hire my own help. I could try one-finger typing, but I don't think that will get me very far in four weeks.' He gave her the beginnings of a smile. 'A friend of mine recommended your agency.'

Hooking her hair behind her ears, she looked pointedly at the white gauze bandage. The sound of his voice wakened memories: it was velvet, edged with steel, with no trace of an Italian accent.

'Your office mentioned why you needed temporary help. Being in a plane crash must have been an terrible experience.'

He didn't comment, and silence engulfed them briefly, until the rattle of porcelain heralded the approach of a trim secretary with a tray. It was set with cups and the other necessities.

'Naturally, we'll have to make the index and so on as we go along.' He indicated towards the pot. 'Coffee?'

The secretary had already withdrawn. 'Yes, please. Shall I pour?'

He nodded, and watched as her slim hands competently poured two cups. She handed him one, black with one spoonful of sugar. She poured another, adding milk, for herself. If he noticed that she already knew how he liked his coffee, he didn't comment. She could have found out that information some-where, in order to impress him.

Rebecca lifted her own cup and took

a sip. The coffee was strong and tasted rough on her tongue. She ought to tell him they weren't strangers. It was bound to emerge eventually. She wished she'd done so straight away.

He set his cup down, and his black eyebrows lifted quizzically. 'I see from your CV that you've a degree?'

Her throat was still raw and dry, despite the welcome coffee. 'Yes, in languages. Our agency aims to provide the best possible secretarial services. My partner, Jennifer, is a qualified accountant, and I'm a professional secretary. We also have some part-timers. Our agency covers almost any kind of office work.'

He looked at her face carefully again. He knew her; she was no stranger. He'd have to sort out who she was before he agreed. A stranger with access to his home would be too risky. 'The doctors recommend that I spend some time at home in Italy. Apparently sun and salt water helps the healing process. We have a family residence on a small island called San Andrea. That means you'll have to come with me. Is that a problem?'

Rebecca swallowed the lump in her throat. 'No, I don't think so. If you engage us, it doesn't make any difference where we work. I presume there's somewhere nearby where I can stay?'

He stated briskly, 'There's plenty of room in the house. There's no suitable lodgings nearby. We're off the beaten track.'

Living in the same house as Luca might be a problem, but it depended how much breathing space he would give her. 'I don't mind, but it will limit your privacy.'

'I value my privacy, and I assure you that we won't step on each other's toes after working hours. Anything else you need to know? I've read through the terms of your contract. It's fine.'

She had to say something. Taking a deep breath, and twisting her hands together, she asked, 'What time do we start working?'

He got up, stood motionless for a moment, and stuck his healthy hand into the pocket of his chinos; the other one hung at his side. 'Eight! We take a short break at lunchtime and carry on till five or six. I reckon we'll finish the book in four or five weeks. I've allowed for unexpected hitches, but you still might have to extend. As soon as the doctor gives me the green light, I intend to return to London. Oh . . . you'll have to sort out your own meals during the day, but you'll take your evening meal with me.' He added, 'It's easier for Franca, our housekeeper, that way.'

'Yes, by all means.' She'd prefer to cater solely for herself, but she couldn't demand it.

'Dinner is usually at nine-thirty.' He noticed how her eyebrows lifted. 'We eat late because of the heat. I'm leaving for San Andrea tomorrow. I'd like you to follow as soon as possible. The office here will make your travel arrangements.'

Rebecca rose. She moistened her lips.

She had to tell him.

He beat her to the post. With a quizzical expression and his dark brows lifted, he asked, 'Miss Summer . . . have we met before? Your face is somehow familiar.'

She took a deep breath, and wished she'd been quicker. 'Yes, we have.' He waited; his brow crinkled. Rebecca continued, 'Eight years ago? At university?'

His mind wandered back through the years; it took him a few seconds, then his eyes widened. He continued to consider her for a few seconds, and then a smile appeared. 'Good Heavens! It's Rebecca! Of course — your eyes and your voice stirred my memory, but you look so different now; and your name didn't ring a bell either!'

She cleared her throat. 'Back then, most people called me Becky, not Rebecca. And I don't suppose you ever heard my surname. Surnames weren't important, were they?'

'You look so different — that's what

really threw me.'

Pink spots coloured her cheeks briefly. 'Not surprising since I weighed a lot more, had bright red hair, and wore too much make-up. Everyone called me Becky even though I disliked it. You always called me Rebecca, even then.' She asked hesitatingly, 'Do you want to change your mind?'

He thrust his hand into his pocket again. 'About hiring you? Why should I? A mate of mine told me your agency is first class, and I need qualified help. Is it really eight years? It seems like a lifetime ago.' A smile lit up his face, and he laughed softly while he ran his free hand through his black curly hair.

Rebecca's answering smile was controlled but genuine. She felt better. 'I'm glad that you don't mind.' She added quickly, 'The agency would like the work. My partner talked to your office about the job when I was out. When I heard who you were, I decided to come for the interview and explain. I didn't know if you'd still want us after you found out I co-own the agency!'

He noted that her eyes were the colour of fine jade. Had he noticed that all those years ago? His mouth curved in lazy appreciation. 'It's okay, Rebecca. It's not a problem.'

Remembering earlier times, he recalled that she was an uncomplicated, hard worker. He'd always enjoyed her company; she was interesting and had decided views on things. He still found it hard to believe that this woman, with her delicate bone structure, wonderful complexion and slim figure, was the same Rebecca he'd once known with the rounded face and generous curves. 'It's a small world, isn't it?'

The colour still heightened the creamy surface of her cheeks. 'Yes, but to be honest, I did wonder why you don't use your own secretary.'

He shrugged. 'I don't have one, because most of the time I don't need one. I'm on the move a lot. I use a laptop and feed that with information. If I need stuff typed, I just email my notes to headquarters, and someone puts it into an acceptable form and emails it back.'

'So why don't you use that method now?'

'Hey, are you trying to do yourself out of a job?' He smiled and a dimple appeared in the cleft of his chin. 'As I said, I need someone on hand. If I used a company secretary, we'd have to find a temporary replacement for her at headquarters. It's more sensible to employ my own temp from the start, especially as I'm paying. By the way, do you know anything about the details of how the business world works?'

'Not more than the average person. Is that a handicap?'

He shrugged his broad shoulders. 'No, not really!' He paused as his thoughts raced. 'Isn't this a crazy coincidence? But a good one. We got on well back then, didn't we?'

Rebecca looked at him but didn't comment.

'We'll catch up on the news when you get to San Andrea.' He took out the

11

bottom sheet of paper and, without reading it, signed his name and handed back the folder with its contents.

Rebecca needed to get away. She needed to catch her breath and attune herself to the knowledge that she'd soon be working for Luca in his family's home in Italy. She looked at her watch. 'Yes, I have another appointment, so if you don't mind . . . ? I'll see you in a day or two, as soon as I've organized things here.'

He tucked his hand under her elbow and walked with her towards the door. 'Fine. Just get in touch with the office and they'll sort out your tickets, etcetera. The fastest way to San Andrea is by plane, and then ferry. I'm looking forward to seeing you again in a couple of days time.'

She gave him a tentative smile and nodded silently. Keeping her rambling thoughts in check, she looked back as she reached the outer door. Luca was still standing there, with his hand on the doorframe. There was something about him that set alarm bells ringing inside her head. She was annoyed that her stomach was swirling wildly, as if she was a star-struck teenager. She must concentrate and remind herself that fate was giving her a chance to get him out of her system. She would grab the opportunity with both hands.

★   ★   ★

Two days later, she arrived on the island of San Andrea without mishap. Giraldo met her from the ferry. On the way to the old farmhouse, driving along stone-lined dusty roads, he explained in good English that he and his wife Franca were responsible for everything to do with the smooth running of the former farm. He pointed out a couple of places of interest along the way, and Rebecca hoped she'd have time to explore the island before she left. When they arrived, he took her straight to meet his wife Franca. She was middle-aged, with a comfortable figure and salt-and-pepper hair drawn into a severe bun. After a welcome drink of lemonade, she took Rebecca to a converted outbuilding, where she would be the sole inhabitant for the length of her stay. Rebecca was relieved and pleased to notice it was separate from the main house.

Franca said, 'Giraldo will come back in an hour to take you to Luca in the main house.'

Rebecca nodded. Alone again, she left her luggage and chose instead to walk to the edge of the cliff that was visible between patches of dull green straggly bushes scattered across the barren ground. It was a short distance away. The heat of the day was fading and cool breezes from the ocean enveloped her when she reached the cliff top. The ocean was a mirror of the red and gold sunset. Rebecca was slightly euphoric when she thought about being here and so close to the sea.

When she returned to the outhouse

she still had a few minutes to freshen up before Giraldo came to show her the shortcut to the walled garden that surrounded the main house. The garden, with its paths, rich succulent plants, and sprinkling of semi-tropical greenery, clearly received more water than the land on the other side of the walls. The house was an old, but modernized, two-storey farmhouse. The original building had been extended and it sprawled comfortably on its chosen spot. Giraldo gestured and left her when they reached the terrace.

Luca stood waiting at the other end. She walked past giant oleanders in muted terracotta pots, and a multitude of comfortable chairs and loungers with blue-and-white cushions. When she reached him, she glanced at a nearby water feature built into the wall of the house. Water bubbled through the mouth of an ancient god into the smooth stone basin below.

Luca's mouth curved into a smile as he followed her movements. The smart linen dress skimmed her slender figure, and her shoulder-length dark hair swung in rhythm with her steps. Her sandaled feet made soft-footed progress over the rough ground. He met her glance and his voice dropped slightly when he said, 'I'm glad you arrived safely. I told Franca to delay dinner until you were here. Let's go in.'

She followed him. The house had thick walls and it was cooler indoors. Luca held her chair at the polished dining table briefly until she was seated, and then pressed a button in the wall next to the marble fireplace. Rebecca wondered if the hearth was ever used at all, but probably the evenings were sometimes chilly in winter. Light music played softly in the background. She was relieved he was dressed casually. It meant that she wouldn't be expected to change every evening. His clothes were classy, but it was the man himself who grabbed her attention, not what he wore.

She left it up to him whether he

wanted to converse or make small talk. At university, they'd been equals, friends with similar interests and mutual acquaintances. Today he was co-owner of an international concern, and she was his temporary employee. She hoped it would work out. There was no guarantee it would. Perhaps he'd changed. She followed his lead when he shook out a snowy white napkin and laid it out of sight on his lap.

He glanced across and asked, 'What have you done since university?'

'Worked and gained experience in several firms, before founding the agency with my partner a couple of years ago!'

Interest and slight amusement showed in his eyes. 'It sounds very clear-cut.'

'Does it? It wasn't easy, and still isn't. There's a lot of rivalry for well-paid temporary secretarial work.'

His dark eyes never left her face. 'There's always competition for anything to do with money.' He gave a barely noticeable shrug. 'No one gives anything for nothing in this life. A friend, Bob Reader, gave me your telephone number. He's a sharp businessman, so that means your agency must be good.'

She nodded and smiled weakly. 'I hope so! You know Bob? He employs us regularly. In fact, we now have quite a few faithful clients. We're still a small-fry agency, but things look promising.'

'You live in London?'

She nodded as Franca came in. Rebecca's mouth watered at the smell of the vegetable soup. She tried some and it tasted wonderful. It was her first meal since that morning. She hoped he didn't notice how hungry she was.

'You haven't married?'

She crumpled the corner of the crisp serviette and lifted her spoon. 'No.' If he wanted more information, she disappointed him.

There was a short silence and then he started to chat again. Luca guessed that she was avoiding the theme of their shared past for some reason. 'Do you live close to your offices? Where?'

'I have a bed-sitter thirty minutes from the office. Most of the time I'm out of the office, working for clients in other parts of London, or out of town . . . '

He broke in with a soft laugh; the dimple creased his chin. 'Or even abroad?'

She relaxed and agreed. 'That hasn't happened very often. Someone did need a foreign language temp once, for a business trip to Paris.'

Franca reappeared, piled the empty soup dishes on a tray, and placed white bowls and fresh gold-edged plates on the table. Luca lifted the lids and a cloud of appetizing smell emerged. He handed her some silver serving spoons.

She took a fat fillet of fish and some vegetables. Picking up her knife and fork to start, she explained, 'Most of our clients are from London. Sometimes I wish I had a car. That would help, especially if I need to rush across the city or reach someone in the suburbs. I'm aiming to buy my own flat, so a car will have to wait. If I work for someone outside London, I use a taxi, or hire a car.'

'Property prices in London are sky-high. What are you hoping to buy?'

'A two-room flat in a less popular area of London. When I pay that off, I can aim for something bigger, somewhere more upmarket. I've been saving ever since the firm took off. Trouble is, the price of property in London goes up constantly, faster than you can save enough.'

He nodded. 'It gets more difficult to find something affordable, even in less popular areas, every year. Do you enjoy your work? Isn't it unpredictable and unnerving . . . having new employers all the time, and a fluctuating income?'

Between forks of delicious fish, she said, 'The unpredictability is what I enjoy. We earn well, when we have work, and I'm never bored. Jennifer and I have learned to budget the earnings and we've learned to keep reserves. Next week, or next month might not be so lucrative.' She wished she could have a second helping of the fish — it tasted wonderful — but she held back.

He looked with pointed interest at the way she was emptying her plate. 'You seem to like Italian food?'

Her colour rose. Was he remembering how she used to eat too much? 'I've always loved Italian food.'

He looked up and sent a crooked smile across the highly polished surface.

A bundle of confused thoughts assailed Rebecca as she watched him butter some crusty bread and take a generous bite. He poured himself coffee and held the pot poised in mid-air with his sound hand. Rebecca lifted her cup and held it towards him. His white shirtsleeves were rolled up to his elbows. She noticed some blotched pale pink patches on the inside of his forearms, and guessed they were the outcome of the crash. She was curious to hear his version of what had happened, but she didn't ask. It was up to him if he wanted to talk about it or not.

He leaned back, sipping the liquid contentedly, and gestured that she should help herself to the honey cakes Franca had just deposited on the table in a big round ceramic dish. 'Get Franca to make a traditional dish for us one day, she has great recipes.'

Franca smiled and said, 'Most are from my grandmother.' She left them, closing the door softly.

Rebecca paused for a moment stirring her coffee with a silver spoon and then tried one of the small cakes. It was extremely sweet, and quite delicious. She longed to suck the sticky remains from her fingertips, but wiped them on her serviette instead.

He cocked his head to one side. 'Aren't you going to ask me what I've been doing since we last met?'

He remembered the young Rebecca when she replied, 'I read the newspapers.'

He gave a hollow laugh. 'With an open mind, I hope?'

'Do you mean about your professional, or your private, life?'

A smile ruffled his mouth. 'Both; but especially about all the ridiculous gossip about my wild jet-setting life-style, and the flamboyant parties.'

Her lashes touched her cheeks briefly. 'You had a colourful social life even at university, didn't you?' She lifted her shoulders. 'You know that the gutter press needs to sell their stories about the rich and the beautiful.' She smiled across the table. 'If a reporter doesn't produce what he wants, the editor probably encourages him to write half-truths just to sell the paper. You seem to be surviving. Unless they print real lies, there's not much you can do to stop them, is there? I don't suppose you care anyway, do you? You know that anyone who plays with fire gets burned.'

His eyes twinkled. He lifted his bandaged hand. 'I've done that without the help of the gutter press.'

Rebecca changed the direction of the conversation. 'Luca ... would you mind if I use the beach? I saw it from the cliff when I went for a quick walk. I don't want to intrude on your privacy, but if you have no objections . . . ?'

He made a brief dismissive gesture, surprised that now he'd given her the opportunity to dig, she hadn't asked more about his private lifestyle. Most people asked lots of questions. 'No, of course not; no-one else is here at the moment, anyway.'

'Is this your house? It's beautiful.'

'No. It's a family home. It used to be a working farm when my grandfather was young. He renovated the buildings as soon as he had spare cash, and extended and improved things several times. My father had the outhouse you're in renovated as a guesthouse last year. It's definitely a perfect spot to relax because it's so isolated and quiet. I love this place more than anywhere else I've ever been. It is where the Barsetti family came from. It is part of my soul.'

'I can understand why. My building is fabulous. Even though it looks basic on the outside, the interior is superbly modern.'

'My father envisioned it as a guesthouse. Sometimes, when we had a big house party, we never had enough room, so he decided to create a couple of extra spaces in the outhouses. He started with yours. There are plans to convert the others one day. I immediately thought it could be a perfect lodging for a temporary secretary, so that she didn't cross my path continually after office hours.'

Rebecca sipped her coffee and met his glance. 'Good from the employee's point of view, too!'

★ ★ ★

His eyebrows lifted and he looked amused. 'Got everything you need?'

He didn't expect any other answer than that he got. 'Yes, thank you! Do Franca and Giraldo live on the premises?'

'Yes. They run everything. The house

is always ready when someone wants to come on the spur of the moment.'

Rebecca wondered if he and his family appreciated what they owned. She made a mental note to ask Franca if Luca used the beach, and when. 'Lucky you! And I envy you the beach very, very much. It's so private and cut-off.'

His white teeth flashed and he sent her a familiar smile. 'I agree. Even though it's fairly small, it's big enough and sheltered. There are dangerous currents once you leave the inlet, so don't overestimate your ability. I take it that you can swim?'

'Yes, but not very well. I promise to be careful.'

'Remember that no one can see you from the house! You'll be swept out to sea unless you're a strong swimmer. Don't take any chances.'

'I won't.'

He passed a hand over his face and added, 'You used to read a lot. If you want to borrow some books, you're welcome to any from the shelves in the sitting room.'

'Thanks!' During university, he'd been confident and uncompromising, and had a constant following of interested female company. It didn't look like he'd changed much. Newspaper articles described him as one of Europe's most eligible bachelors, and women pursued him constantly. Some described him as arrogant. He wasn't. Even in the past, he was reserved, but only because he wanted to be accepted for what he was, and not because he came from an affluent background. Rebecca had met several arrogant men via her work. She knew the difference between arrogance and reticence. She emptied her cup, put her serviette on the table, and pushed back the chair. Politely, he rose too.

'The meal was very good; thank you!'

'Don't thank me; thank Franca! Your office is the first door on the right, top of the stairs. We'll meet at eight.' He didn't try to delay her. Only time would tell if he'd made the right choice. Until then, he'd keep things on a friendly but professional footing.

She gave him a hesitant smile. 'Goodnight.'

'Goodnight, Rebecca.'

★   ★   ★

The door closed. He mused on how he was breaking his self-imposed rule never to employ someone he knew. Business and pleasure didn't mix well. He felt a twinge of anxiety.

But Rebecca was different. He'd always liked her quiet self-confidence, and her interesting, intelligent personality. What could go wrong? He tucked a newspaper from the sideboard under his arm and headed for the sitting room.

2

Back inside her new home, Rebecca leaned against the door for a moment. She tried, but couldn't shut Luca out of her thoughts. His name continued to circle her mind, and the years fell away.

In her university days, she'd shared a flat with Gaynor, a drama student. One evening, Gaynor persuaded her to come along to rehearsal — they needed behind-the-scenes helpers.

That first evening, after she'd shaken the rain from her umbrella, she looked around and saw Luca for the first time. Many of the faces were new to her, but his handsome features captured her imagination immediately, and she studied him longer than usual. He was busy talking to some people on the other side of the room.

Jenny grinned knowingly as she watched Rebecca's face. 'That's Luca.

He's co-heir to the Barsetti shipping and banking dynasty. Dishy, isn't he? He's actually a very nice guy in spite of all that money. Luca volunteered to find us sponsors, and he's good at it. He helps with the sound and lighting, and handles the boring administration work no one else wants to do. Despite the fact that he's Italian, he's surprisingly good at calming shattered egos and irate producers. Come on, I'll introduce you' She dragged an embarrassed Rebecca along with her.

'Luca, got a moment? I've brought reinforcements. This is my friend Rebecca.'

Luca's smile flashed briefly; it was dazzling against his olive skin. Something like a shockwave hit Rebecca as she met his eyes. Her cheeks coloured, and she made an effort to remain cool.

'Hi, Rebecca! Welcome! Are you another budding actress?'

Rebecca's eyes widened. 'Heavens, no! Gaynor said help was needed backstage.'

With a connoisseur's gaze, he decided that the bright ginger curls tumbling to her shoulders didn't quite match the colour of her heavily contoured eyes, or the creamy tone of her skin. Redheads generally had very pale skins. The colour of her eyebrows was wrong for a redhead, too. 'Anything in particular? Lighting, costumes, scenery?'

'It wouldn't be safe to put me within arm's length of anything electrical. Something more innocuous and middle-of-the-road would suit better!'

He liked the sound of her voice and the sparkle in her eyes. Her friendly face with its rounded contours was outgoing and confident. He nodded. 'Why not give things the once-over tonight? Then, if you're still interested, we'll sort something definite out next week. We need all the help we can get — organizing the wardrobe; helping with make-up; publicity and sponsoring, etcetera.' He turned to Jenny. 'Hey! Mart's asking for you — they've started rehearsing scene three.'

Jenny scurried away, and Rebecca watched as she ran up the wooden steps onto the stage. A small group of people with dog-eared scripts stood in the centre in a half-circle, listening to a short, middle-aged man. Someone shouted to Luca from across the room. He gave Rebecca a smile and moved away. Rebecca escaped to the anonymity of the shadows, and spent the rest of the evening watching as she worked.

She enjoyed herself. Luca crossed her field of vision sometimes, and she watched him surreptitiously during the coffee break. Even though he was only dressed in washed-out jeans and a simple dark blue fisherman's sweater, he was the most attractive man she'd ever met. His Mediterranean ancestry was apparent in his classical features and swarthy complexion. She yanked the capacious T-shirt down over her jeans, and wished she hadn't eaten the extra portion of lasagne last night. Although she didn't realize it at the time, it was love at first sight.

A year later, by the time she'd helped with two plays, they had a unique relationship. She always envied his various girlfriends, but none of them lasted. Their platonic friendship did. She had no illusions about herself. Why should someone like Luca, who could pick and choose, think twice about a girl who disguised her chunky figure with shapeless outfits from second-hand shops, and dyed her long unruly hair bright ginger to divert attention from her less-than-perfect shape? People who liked her accepted her for what she was. They liked her honesty and uncomplicated, friendly personality. Sometimes she intentionally brought a boyfriend along to rehearsals, just to show Luca that other men liked her, despite all the surplus kilos.

Luca was studying business management and economics. When his finals loomed, he handed his job over to someone else. The new chap kept things ticking over, but Rebecca never went to rehearsals with the same kind of elation. She missed Luca.

Their paths seldom crossed after that: a wave, a quick chat on the pavement, or a smile in passing was all. She heard that he'd passed his exams with honours, but she didn't offer congratulations. Their paths had crossed, then they'd moved apart again for ever — or so she'd thought until recently. Her partner had handled the initial negotiations for this job. Perhaps if she'd been involved from the beginning she would have refused outright.

Fate had brought them together again; she was sharing his working day, eating at his table, and living in his home. Rebecca threw back her shoulders. She would bury those dizzy teenage daydreams at last. She was an independent, ambitious, and attractive woman these days. There was no reason to feel dazed by Luca Barsetti anymore.

For a few days, it felt almost bizarre to be working with him again, but they both had a very professional attitude, so things went smoothly. He'd done a lot of preparatory work, and by the end of the first week, they'd got through the rough draft of the first four chapters.

They slipped back into a companionable partnership. Rebecca didn't squander any time reminding him about the past. They did relax more during the evening meal, and their discussions roamed back and forth across a wide range of topics and subjects. Sometimes they agreed, other times they had opposing views. Sometimes Rebecca felt time had stood still, and they were back in that gaunt rehearsal room, solving the world's problems and playing politics after all the others had left. One thing hadn't changed: unconsciously, they both kept their personal life out of their conversations.

Rebecca tried to keep up her walking routine before she went to work. She'd started doing so several years ago; with that, along with developing better eating habits, she'd gradually reduced weight and changed her general appearance.

She walked in the fresh morning air across faint pathways that criss-crossed semi-arid fields. She got to know the surrounding area better. One morning, on her way back to her home, she met Luca. He wore a white towelling robe and had a towel round his neck. His jet-black hair was damp, rivulets of seawater trickled down his neck, and his face was shadowed with a morning beard.

The world was silent and the landscape bathed in the yellowish-gold of the morning sun as it emerged from the mists. Her appearance surprised him, but he recovered swiftly.

'Another early bird?'

Rebecca made a mental note to avoid this path to the beach in future: he was entitled to his privacy. 'So it seems.'

He studied her slim figure in pale cotton running gear and clumsy-looking shoes. 'You jog?'

'No, I walk. Whenever I can, provided I'm not too lazy! I don't manage it every day; sometimes it's too much of a hassle.'

He nodded. She was waiting for him

to move on, but he was in an inquisitive mood. 'What else do you do in your spare time these days?'

'Not much. You know sport was never high on my list of favourite pastimes.'

'I meant generally, apart from sport.'

She looked down, her dark lashes sweeping her cheeks, before she met his glance and answered. 'Oh, just the usual things: art exhibitions, the theatre, pop concerts, classical music; and I sketch a little, too — for my own amusement.' His eyebrows lifted. 'Nothing professional. It just helps me to relax.' She decided to be polite. 'And you?'

He stuck his hands into the roomy pockets of his robe. 'I live in London most of the time, and I still enjoy the theatre. I read a lot, and I enjoy sport whenever I can fit it in to my schedule — tennis, sailing, climbing. At the moment I'm limited to swimming.' His eyes flickered for a moment. Rebecca guessed the plane accident was still a sensitive subject. He added, 'Luckily, salt water has healing properties.'

He studied her face: it glowed from the exercise, and her eyes sparkled like rough emeralds beneath finely arched eyebrows. A straying breeze ruffled the auburn strands of hair escaping from the sweatband round her forehead.

'I tried it once too,' he continued, 'but gave it up because I found it too boring.'

Her thoughts were wandering and she hadn't been concentrating properly. 'Sorry, what did you say?'

'Walking . . . I found it boring!'

Her eyes flashed irritation. 'Perhaps it wasn't exclusive enough?'

He looked at her in surprise. 'No, it wasn't challenging enough; I like competition. Am I a social snob, just because I don't enjoy walking?'

She stared at him, and was mad with herself; he was right. It was unfair to attack him like that, and to try putting him in a bad light. She was over-reacting because she wanted reasons to forget him. She tried to backpedal. 'Sorry, I didn't mean to be bitchy.

You're right. It doesn't really matter what you do, as long as it's for fun.'

The friendliness was back in his expression. The tanned skin creased as he smiled, and the corner of his mouth twitched. 'I take it that we are still talking about sport?' His smile had a touch of eroticism.

She swallowed hard. 'What else?'

He pulled the towel from his neck. 'Oh . . . before I forget, my brother's family are coming on Friday for the weekend. It makes no difference to our work, and you'll still come across to the main house for the evening meal.'

'Just say the word if you'd prefer to be private . . . '

'I just explained you're not in the way, Rebecca. Do you want me to dictate it, so that you can pin a copy to the noticeboard?'

She coloured slightly. 'Of course not! Oh, by the way, am I free on the weekend?'

'Sure; we're on schedule so far! Enjoy yourself!' He looked at his watch. 'We'd better get dressed.' Turning abruptly, he left her standing and strolled off towards the house.

As she wandered back to the outhouse, she persuaded herself that her interest and fascination would fade after a while. Rebecca ducked beneath the branches of a group of lemon trees bordering the outhouse's small patio, and a few minutes later she was under the shower.

* * *

The first signs of the visitors were the squeaky voices of children somewhere nearby, then she saw them, strolling aimlessly side-by-side through the olive trees. They were neatly dressed and the boy scuffed the ground with his trainers, leaving a cloud of fine dust behind him as he went. Rebecca was sitting on an old drystone wall, reading. She smiled at the little girl and received a shy smile in return. 'Hello!'

Glad of any kind of distraction, the

little girl replied. 'Hello . . . who are you?'

She was already very pretty, with jet-black curly hair hanging down her back. She had dark lashes and dark grey eyes. The boy was dark, too. He was older and taller, with bold, questioning eyes. His expression told Rebecca that strange women weren't very welcome to him.

'I'm Rebecca, your uncle's temporary secretary.'

'I'm Gabriella, and this is my brother Filipo.' She looked at Rebecca with a puzzled expression. 'What does temporary mean?'

'Don't be daft, Gabriella! It means she's only here for a while. I want to see the donkeys.' He reminded Rebecca of Luca: the same dark eyes, high cheekbones, stubborn chin — and the same desire to control and manage.

Gabriella's lips puckered. 'I'm not daft; and don't boss me around! You pretend you know everything, but you don't, so there!'

Rebecca didn't want to intervene but she felt sorry for them. She indicated the jug on the patio table nearby. 'Are you thirsty? Would you like some lemonade?'

'No, thanks! I've just had some from Franca.' In a high-pitched voice, Gabriella explained, 'We want to go swimming, but they're too busy talking. We're not allowed to go on our own!'

Rebecca thought briefly about the pile of underwear she was planning to wash. She liked children. 'How about me? I'll come with you, if you promise to behave and your parents agree.'

Gabriella clapped her hands. 'Oh, really? Come on, Filipo, let's ask.'

Filipo grinned at Rebecca, all his former indifference forgotten. 'That would be super!'

An hour later, Rebecca sat and watched them swimming parallel to the edge of the water. They could both swim well, but they'd been told not to head out to sea. Rebecca still kept a watchful eye on them.

Thrashing around wildly in the water, Gabriella shouted, 'Rebecca, come and join us!'

She got up and brushed the rough, dry sand from her bottom. Secretly, she was glad because her skin was already tender from too much sun. She envied friends who tanned overnight. She threw her shirt onto the sand, and joined them.

A little while later, Luca and his brother descended the rough steps cut into the face of the cliff. He paused for a moment to watch the small figures in the azure waters below. He indicated towards them with his chin. 'There they are; having a great time, by the look of it.'

The two men resembled each other, although Marco was older, broader, a few centimetres shorter, and his dark hair was tightly waved. 'So it seems.' He paused and turned to Luca. 'Have you come to terms with what happened yet?'

Luca shrugged, stuck his bandaged hand in his pocket, and stared out to sea. 'More or less! The ribs are mending; the burns are healing. Actually, most days I feel a bit of a fraud wasting time here when I could be in the thick of things in London.'

Marco held up a hand. 'You are not wasting time! The doctors said you need time to adjust mentally to what happened, and the burns also need time to heal properly. You can afford to take time off. When did you last have a holiday? The work won't go away, and I'm sure that you're keeping yourself informed about anything really important.'

'Of course. The internet is a godsend.'

'Follow other people's advice for once.'

Luca nodded. 'I'd get bored if I had nothing to do. Writing this book keeps me sane.'

Marco laughed and then paused, looking questioningly at his brother. 'Be honest: how do you feel?'

Luca gave him a crooked smile. 'I never thought I'd be in a crash; who does? The pilot died, I survived. That bothers me most of all, because he was married with a small daughter. If one of us had to die, why him and not me?'

'There's no answer to that question; don't dwell on it. Don't feel guilty. Life isn't always black and white! Perhaps it's the gift of a second life for you. Accept it, and move on. It wasn't your fault, not your choice, not your wish; it was just fate.'

'Hmm, but I keep thinking about it all the time.'

'That's natural. You'll put it behind you eventually, though, I'm sure. Other things will grab your attention and take over.'

With his gaze on the expanse of the sea ahead of them, Luca murmured, 'The crash made me more aware than ever that money and power aren't really important, are they?'

Luca laughed softly. 'They're not irrelevant either, are they? As far as I'm concerned, Chiara, the children, the family, and the business are very important — in that order. You need money and influence to lead the sort of lives we do. You know that yourself.'

'But we're so rich and influential we can make or break people — or even companies — at the drop of a hat. We act pretty ruthlessly sometimes, don't we?' Sea breeze ruffled his hair and Luca waited.

'Hey! We're not in it for pleasure. Our competitors are just as ruthless! It doesn't mean we need to employ callous or unfair tactics, or destroy someone just for fun. Successful business isn't just about gaining power, riches, and control — that's the easy part! It's about how you use them once they're yours. You have to retain your personal integrity while swimming in a sea full of hungry sharks. If you resist the temptation to wipe out a competitor for the wrong reasons, you sleep easy. If you destroy someone just for fun, it will boomerang. Money corrupts, if you let it! Grandpa never used cut-throat methods; he gave his competitors a fair fight. We've been trained to do the same, haven't we? Most of his business acquaintances were lifelong friends, even though they were also competitors. His opponents respected him, and he even kept his private life intact too.'

Luca nodded and smiled. 'That was particularly impressive. I envy him. The press hound me every step I take.'

Marco laughed softly. 'Because you're still on the market. If you were married, they'd target someone else. Find yourself a wife!'

Luca laughed. ' The older I get, the choosier I am. You were lucky. You found Chiara early on, and you suited each other from day one.'

Marco nodded. 'I was a lot younger then than you are now; so get your skates on!' He paused and looked seriously at his brother. 'No, I don't really mean that. Finding the right woman is the most important thing you'll ever do.' He stared out at an aeroplane skimming across the horizon. 'What about flying? Does it still scare you?'

Luca looked ill at ease. 'Yes, like hell.

I thought it was a temporary hitch; but I break out in a sweat every time I think of it.'

'That's bound to sort itself out eventually. If not, get professional help. It's early days yet. I suspect that it's a perfectly normal reaction!' Marco watched the figures moving in the water. 'I'm always there for you, Luca. If I can do anything, just say the word!'

Luca shook his head silently. 'Not at the moment, but thanks! We'd better collect the children before Chiara comes storming after us.'

Rebecca saw them crossing the pebbles at the top of the beach. The children raced towards the two men, leaving Rebecca still dripping at the edge of the water.

Gabriella's voice drifted back. 'Daddy! You've come for a swim?'

He laughed, his dark eyes embracing the children. He looked at Gabriella's pleading eyes and folded her tiny hands between his. 'Not today, sweetheart! I will tomorrow, promise! Luca and I came to fetch you, and make sure you're not annoying Miss — . . . ?'

'Rebecca Summer, but you can call her Rebecca,' Luca said firmly, his eyes moving from the children to Rebecca and back again. He ruffled Filipo's hair. His brother looked at him in surprise. Luca's eyes were expressionless as he explained, 'We were at university together.'

'Really?' Marco smiled and looked at Rebecca.

Rebecca joined them and caught the edge of the conversation. 'It was a fluke of fate! We last saw each other eight years ago.'

Marco eyed them both speculatively. 'I'm sure that's his loss, not yours!' He stuck out his hand. 'Hello, Rebecca! I'm Marco. I hope my two have behaved themselves?'

Rebecca laughed softly, shook his hand, and was glad that he was so friendly.

'We have, and you've enjoyed yourself too, haven't you, Rebecca?' Gabriella said quickly.

'Absolutely.' Rebecca smiled at them indulgently.

'Your mother is waiting for you to unpack your suitcases, and have a shower.' The children greeted the news with a groan. 'No arguments! Tomorrow you can do what you like, but not if you disobey now.' That prospect was a nightmare; they picked up their towels from the nearby rocks and ran. Their father turned to her.

'Thanks for looking after them; it was kind of you.' His polite smile was open and generous; like Luca, he had regular, attractive teeth. She admired the way he took charge of the children with quiet assurance.

'No problem! They both speak such good English; I'm impressed.'

'Ah! That's my grandmother's influence! I expect you know that she's English?'

Rebecca's eyebrows lifted. 'No. I didn't.'

'Everyone in the family speaks English. When she's around, we never speak Italian, do we Luca?'

'No.' He decided he ought to be just

as charming. His smile deepened, and under the scrutiny of his gaze, Rebecca couldn't concentrate properly.

Rebecca focused on Marco. 'It sounds like she's a very interesting woman.'

Marco nodded. 'My grandfather acted like a macho man sometimes, but he wasn't. She influenced him constantly from the day they married, until he died. They had a wonderful marriage, full of fireworks and love, affection and respect. It was always a pleasure to be with them. Unfortunately he died three years ago.'

'But he left her with lots of good memories. If they were married for such a long time, perhaps that will help her to cope with life on her own.'

He nodded again in silent agreement. 'We hope so. Perhaps you'll meet her! Is she coming, Luca?'

'Not sure! She loves San Andrea, because Grandpa came from here, but she doesn't like travelling much any-more.'

Marco added, 'And she still misses Grandfather dreadfully.'

Luca agreed. 'Although she'll never admit it.'

Rebecca leaned down to reach for her shirt. Luca's eyes raked boldly over the slim compact figure in her red bikini, and ended by staring at the cap of her dark hair, glistening like polished wood in the afternoon sun. Marco glanced briefly at her too, and then noticed the expression on his brother's face. He looked at Rebecca and studied her more closely, grinning knowingly to himself.

Luca was quicker than Rebecca. He picked up her shirt and held it out expectantly.

She straightened, and Luca's gaze dropped from her thick-lashed green eyes to her shoulders, then to her small, high breasts. She coloured at the implication in his eyes. Her heart skipped a beat and her pulse increased noticeably. She cleared her throat. 'Thanks. She slipped her arms inside the shirt, and their hands met accidentally. Rebecca managed to control the impulse to jerk away She was bewildered that such brief contact could shake her equilibrium. She was a sensible adult now, not easily impressed. She wasn't a naïve girl. Any attraction she felt for him was buried in the past. She'd find out how to ignore it, and then she'd be able to erase him from her memory.

3

Rebecca made an extra effort that evening. She changed into a white dress cut on misleadingly simple lines that had cost more than she cared to remember, but which always made her feel wonderful. When she joined the others in the dining room, Luca studied her longer than necessary, but didn't comment. He introduced her to his sister-in-law. Chiara, Marco's wife, was friendly, and it was pleasant to have the children and another woman at the table.

Sometimes they forgot she was there, and spoke Italian until someone — usually Luca — remembered. She didn't mind because the atmosphere was so friendly. Franca's food was always good, but this evening it was even more special. The meal ended with oval-shaped almond biscuits with iced coffee for the adults and milkshakes for the children. Filipo and Melissa were in a holiday mood, although their parents controlled any silliness when they got too excited. Rebecca left them after coffee, even though they invited her to stay.

Next morning, she went for a swim; later than Luca's usual time, but before she expected to see anyone else. Afterwards, she went to find Franca. She was preparing breakfast and gestured her towards a chair.

'Morning, Franca! I know that you're very busy.' Franca's dark eyes twinkled and she pushed a plate with olives and local cheese within Rebecca's reach. Rebecca couldn't resist; she ate a handful of juicy olives and sucked the liquid from her fingertips. 'Is Giraldo going into town today by any chance?'

Franca nodded. 'He goes to the port to fetch fish for soup.'

'Oh, good! Can I go with him? I'd like to look around the town.'

Franca nodded. 'You are back for

dinner? You want Giraldo to fetch you?'

Rebecca shook her head. 'No. I'll eat something there, and catch the bus back later. I've seen where the bus stops, up on the roadway. Giraldo can show me where to catch it from the port.'

Franca's expression was critical. She didn't believe in too much female independence. But she didn't comment, just said, 'If you go shopping, Giraldo can bring it back with him, then you won't need to carry it around all day.'

'If he's there long enough; I won't keep him hanging about.'

Franca looked puzzled. 'Hanging about? Why should he hang somewhere!'

Rebecca smiled at the complexities of language. Franca's English was very good, but evidently some jargon was still a mystery. 'Oh, I just meant he shouldn't wait for me.'

Franca nodded, and then looked at Rebecca thoughtfully. 'Come to tell us you are back.'

Rebecca sighed. 'I live in the middle of London, Franca, on my own! I can take care of myself . . . but, if it makes you feel better, I'll knock at your window.' She rose and patted the older woman's arm.

Franca liked this English woman. She didn't expect them to serve her incessantly. She was different to a lot of their visitors. She was too independent; but then, today women were generally very confident. Franca preferred the old days when women were more obedient. She wasn't sure if she liked the way things had changed since her youth. Nowadays young girls weren't as submissive. She crossed herself and got on with her work.

Giraldo smiled a toothy smile when she got into the Jeep. Stocky, in his fifties, with dark skin, twinkling eyes, and an abundance of black wavy hair greying at the temples, he pulled a red kerchief from his pocket and dabbed at his forehead. 'Do you find it's warm here compared to England?'

'Yes, but I love the sunshine. Your English, and Franca's, is really good

— where did you learn?'

He shrugged his broad shoulders, and his polo shirt settled comfortably again over the slight bulge of his stomach. 'We both lived in London for a while and helped my brother run his restaurant, but we didn't like the cold and all the rain, so we came back to Italy.'

The Jeep bounced its way along the bumpy twisting track away from the house, on the rocky promontory over-looking the sea. Ancient olive trees with thick, gnarled trunks and lemon trees were sprinkled everywhere along the way; their leaves shook as the Jeep sped past. The road, when they reached it, was tarmacked, but Giraldo knew of other shortcuts down to the port where the ferries came and went. She liked the appearance of the sun-beaten scenery as the car hurtled past a landscape dotted with stone walls and white-washed buildings.

'How long have you lived on the island?' she asked, pitching her voice over the drone of the engine.

'Ever since London! The previous caretakers retired and we took over. It used to be a farm like all the others until old Mr Barsetti bought a fishing trawler and established the shipping company. The family is into all kinds of businesses these days: clothes, oil, citrus products, banking, construction work. When Mr Barsetti started to make money, he moved the headquarters to the mainland and rented out the land here to a local farmer. He extended and modernized the farmhouse and turned it into a family retreat. Most of the land is still rented out to adjoining farmers. We still make our own olive oil, though; the press is in one of the outhouses.'

Rebecca was too curious not to ask about Luca's plane crash. Luca hadn't volunteered any information. 'You told me Luca was in a plane crash the day you met me. What happened?'

Giraldo gripped the steering wheel like the horns of a rampaging bull. 'Didn't you read about it? The company jet had to make an emergency landing, and the fuselage broke into two on touchdown. Luca was thrown clear of the wreckage. He was knocked unconscious, but when he came round, the plane was on fire. He managed to pull the pilot out, although they found out later the poor devil had died instantly, then the fuel tanks exploded. Luca got some burns and broke a couple of ribs. It was sheer luck that he wasn't killed.'

She flinched inwardly. She was glad when Giraldo's voice told her the port was round the next corner. Rebecca concentrated on the town hugging the shoreline as it came into sight.

As soon as he parked the car in the shadow of a wall, they walked down a cobbled alleyway to the main street. A ferry had just arrived; the crew was unloading the cars and the passengers. The harbour was congested and very busy. Clusters of people hurried past, chattering loudly and laden with bags, suitcases and boxes. The arrival was tying the small quayside in knots. There was a ferry from the mainland twice a day, and also a high-speed catamaran in summer. She had a feeling she was on holiday, even though she was here to work. Giraldo showed her where to buy groceries in a small shop down a narrow side street. She bought some fresh bread, yoghurt and goat's cheese, and returned to wait by the Jeep for Giraldo. When he returned, he bore a newspaper parcel, out of which a fish tail was hanging.

She held up her purchases. 'Will you take these things back for me, please?'

'Of course. You're sure you want to catch the bus back? It's no trouble to fetch you.'

'Thanks, but I'll find my own way home when I'm ready.' She tilted her head and smiled.

He shrugged understandingly, and wiped the back of his neck with the giant handkerchief and pointed across the road. 'The bus stops over there. The service is pretty good. There should be a timetable, but if not, ask. Most people understand English, because of the tourists. Know how to find the way back from the main road?'

Rebecca nodded. 'I'll just follow the track. It's not far; I'll be fine.'

She waited until he began his climb away from the town in a cloud of dust. She turned away and sighed contentedly before she set off to explore the small town.

Small cube-shape houses nestled along the crescent-shaped beach. The air was salty and full of aromatic smells. There was a narrow strip of land bordering the beach where shaded tables and chairs stood in tidy order. Waiters dodged back and forth with trays of drinks and ice cream. She sauntered along the shoreline, loving the fresh sea breezes and bright sunlight. The odd assemblage of walls, terraces, courtyards and alleyways was incongruous, but in complete harmony with the environment.

Rebecca reached the end of the bay and then retraced her steps. She was thirsty, and walked towards one of the tables bordering the beach. She bumped into a tall, lean man with ash-blond hair. Simultaneous attempts at an apology made them laugh.

'You're British?'

She nodded. 'I'm from London. And you?'

'Salisbury. On holiday?'

'No. I'm working here.'

'Lucky you! By the way, my name is Peter, Peter Stanley.'

'And I'm Rebecca Summer — Rebecca!'

'If you work here, you must know the island well?'

She laughed softly. 'No, I don't! In fact, this is my first day off since I arrived.'

He paused, looked at the empty tables nearby, and asked hesitatingly, 'How about a drink?'

It was a guileless invitation, and fitted Rebecca's intentions anyway. 'Why not?'

They choose a table directly facing the sea. Rebecca instinctively liked Peter's quiet face. He ordered them iced coffee and relaxed. Stretching his back and offering his face to the sun, he said, 'Isn't this a wonderful little place? The island isn't very big, but it isn't spoiled by too many tourists. What do you do for a living?' His fair hair flopped onto his forehead.

Salty breezes ruffled her own hair, and it danced around her face; she tried vainly to clamp it behind her ears. 'I'm a secretary; and you?'

'Teacher. Classics master at a boarding school.'

'Then you must find all this Italian history fascinating.'

'Yes. I usually spend my holidays in Italy or Greece every year. I love both countries. Their history has always fascinated me.'

Glasses of iced coffee arrived, and when the cold liquid coated her mouth it felt wonderfully refreshing and smooth. They talked easily, and when the glasses were empty, he said, 'I was on my way to visit the local church.'

'Is it very special? Where is it?'

'There are a couple of churches on

this island, but the local one does get a special mention in my guidebook.' He paused for a moment. 'Like to come? Or perhaps you'd rather look around this place for a while?' He noted her surprise. 'Or am I jumping the gun?'

She shook her head. 'I'd like to come, if you're sure I won't get in the way.'

'The church is up the hill in the old part of the town.' Noticing her amused expression, he said, 'What's the matter? Have I said something funny?'

She laughed softly. 'No. I came from that direction!' Rebecca didn't usually accept invitations from complete strangers. Perhaps it had something to do with the weather or the surroundings, or perhaps it was just that she intuitively trusted him.

He called the waiter and, despite her protests, paid the bill, exchanging a few sentences in Italian as he did.

She hoisted her bag into position. 'I'm impressed! Is Italian difficult?'

He shrugged. 'If you had Latin in

school, it's fairly easy. I always try to hold simple conversations, and when people notice you're making an effort it breaks down the barriers.'

He had a hired car; it was parked in a nearby street. The sun was high, and the road climbed upwards and towards a hilltop community. After the more static heat of the port, the cooler air up on the hillside was very welcome. They used Peter's guidebook to find the church in the busy little town. They studied the exterior, and then the interior, of the eighteenth-century building. He read information from the guidebook, and they wandered around the cobbled streets and alleyways afterwards.

The day passed quickly. They shared a light meal, in a restaurant with a lovely view across the hills, before wandering again afterwards. Rebecca decided he was a genuinely pleasant man. When the sun began to weaken, she looked at her watch and thought about finding a bus, and about the walk to get her back to the farm from the road.

'I think I have to go! Thanks for a lovely day. It was really nice meeting you, Peter.' She put out her hand and smiled.

He took it, and held it a second or two longer than necessary. 'Are you doing anything on Tuesday or Wednesday? If not, perhaps we could meet again for a meal?'

Rebecca was pleased. It would be a digression; help her forget her boss for a couple of hours. She'd hoped she would have already conquered her interest in him by now, but that hadn't happened. 'Yes, I'd like that.'

His face brightened. 'Good! I'll drive you back home now, if you like. It will save you getting the bus, and I'll know where to pick you up. Shall we say Tuesday?' He drove with more care, and less speed, than Giraldo, and they came to a gentle stop in front of the outhouse.

Rebecca didn't see Luca, returning from an excursion across the fields with Filipo in tow and Gabriella on his shoulders. Gabriella spotted Rebecca. 'Look, Uncle Luca! There's Rebecca. Who's that with her?'

Luca glanced through the shifting branches of the trees, and eyed the two of them, before looking ahead again. 'No idea! I'm sure your mother would tell you that curiosity killed the cat.' The idea of Rebecca in the company of a strange man surprised — and then annoyed — him. Perhaps she already knew him. Rebecca surely wasn't the type to begin casual relationships.

He felt a twinge in the pit of his stomach; it unnerved him. It was none of his business. She was entitled to spend her free time as she pleased. He must be missing the bright lights more than he realized.

'Let's go, your mother will be wondering where you are!'

*　*　*

Chiara came down to the beach next morning, just as Rebecca was leaving.

'Hello, Rebecca!'

'Morning, Mrs Barsetti.'

'Oh, Chiara, please. If my children call you Rebecca, so can I.'

Rebecca smiled softly. She eyed the two children already pulling sunshades from a pile in the shelter of a nearby recess in the rock. 'Making themselves useful, I see.'

'They will do absolutely anything to get someone to come to the beach with them.'

Rebecca picked up her towel, and rubbed her head and body energetically, before she finally wrapped it around her hips like a sarong. 'That's perfectly understandable, isn't it?' Her hair stood in disorderly russet wisps around her head like a halo.

'Of course! If I read my book here or on the terrace, it makes no difference. I'm hoping Marco will join me soon. The two men have started discussing business again.' Her forehead wrinkled in frustration. 'I wish they wouldn't all the time, but I can't stop them.'

'I expect it's inevitable when you manage a big business. Do you come from the same kind of background as your husband? Or am I being too inquisitive?'

'Good heavens, no! My family are 'comfortably off', as they say, but not rich.'

'I expect that being part of a prominent family isn't always easy?'

'No. But it has lots of compensations.' Chiara paused and sank back into the soft upholstery. She smiled up at Rebecca. 'I must say, it's nice to have someone of my own generation to talk to. Franca is absolutely wonderful with the children, but we have nothing in common. I think she disapproves of me because I'm too modern. She told us you were out yesterday? Did you enjoy yourself?'

'Yes. I explored a bit. The island is very picturesque, isn't it?'

'I suppose it is, from a tourist's point of view. It's a lifetime since I came here for the first time. My family are from the mainland.'

'I'll be off, and leave you in peace.'

'Not much chance of that with those two over there! Oh, my parents-in-law and Marco's grandmother are coming this afternoon, so the house will be full. You'll meet them at dinner.'

Rebecca eyed the other woman quietly. 'I can easily cater for myself. I don't need to intrude on family gatherings.'

Chiara looked genuinely surprised. 'We all bring friends or acquaintances here from time to time. There's often someone new at the table. Anyway, Marco told me you know Luca from long ago, so that qualifies you as a friend in a loose sense, doesn't it?'

Rebecca shrugged and smiled. 'I don't think that a student friendship a long time ago qualifies me for extra privileges!'

Chiara waved her hands in the air dismissively. 'It's not a privilege. Sharing the evening meal is part of your contract, isn't it? Do come! I have a selfish motive; it will stop Marco and

Luca talking business all evening!'

Rebecca smiled and signalled her agreement with a nod. 'If you put it like that — all right, I'll come.'

4

Rebecca came through the main entrance, and adjusted a shoulder strap before she got ready to walk towards the dining room. She was used to meeting new people all the time because of her job, but it still didn't come easily to her.

She heard the click of high-heeled shoes, and looked up to see a tall, slim woman descending the curved stair-case. Her face was very familiar, but Rebecca wasn't immediately able to pinpoint her name. The woman paused for a fraction of a second when she saw Rebecca, but then continued to descend; her long painted fingernails drifted lightly over the surface of the banister. The diaphanous folds of the dress flowed in lavender waves around her ultra-slim body. She was exquisite, with huge amethyst eyes and thick jet-black hair that bounced on her shoulders with every step.

When they met, Rebecca smiled at her in a friendly way. 'Good evening! I'm Rebecca Summer, Mr Barsetti's temporary secretary.'

The violet eyes skimmed calculatingly over Rebecca's appearance before the woman inclined her face condescendingly. She said, 'Yes, Luca mentioned you were here when we arrived.'

Suddenly, Rebecca knew who she was — Antonia Lorenzo! Photos of the famous Italian model graced the pages of all the glossy magazines.

Miss Lorenzo led the way toward the dining room. Sounding slightly patronizing, she murmured, 'Dinner will be a little late. I wasn't expected, and Luca's grandmother has decided to have something on a tray in her room this evening. She's tired from the journey. It seems there's lots of confusion in the kitchen, and the table settings have to be reorganised.'

Rebecca sympathised silently with Franca. Franca always tried to have everything in perfect order. An unexpected guest would always defeat her carefully prepared plans.

The meal went well, even if Rebecca didn't contribute much to the conversation.

Next morning, she was already busy typing from the dictating machine when the door opened and Luca came in. She hadn't expected to see him, and for some stupid reason his sudden appearance made her heartbeat spiral. She took off her headphones.

'Got enough work to keep you busy?'

She looked up at him. His white shirt was rolled to the elbows, and the sun had already darkened his tan. 'Yes. When I've finished typing, I still have to do the corrections on the sections you've already read and checked.'

'Good. I'll try to dictate some more during the day, but at the moment things are a bit disorganised because of extra people all over the house. It's hard to find a quiet corner.'

'I can imagine.' She turned her attention back to the keyboard, expecting him to disappear as quickly as he'd come.

His voice was firm. 'Rebecca! I realise that it was well-meant, but there was no reason for you to scurry away after the meal yesterday.' He eyed her carefully and tipped his head to one side.

She reddened slightly. 'I . . . I didn't want to intrude. I assumed that your family, and your visitor, would like a bit of privacy.'

He interrupted whatever else she intended to say. 'When other people are here, it doesn't affect us. We have to stick to our schedule; otherwise, we won't make it on time. That doesn't mean that once the meal is over you have to gulp your coffee and run. You're entitled to relax and enjoy your evening meal in peace — that is part of your contract.'

The beginning of a smile touched the corners of her mouth. 'I didn't gulp, and I didn't scurry or run, Luca. I hope I withdrew with dignity.'

She succeeded in disarming him for a second; his facial expression relaxed. 'You know what I mean. Enjoy the meal without any hassle! I'll look in later, but I'll be somewhere in the house if you need me.'

Did she need him? The colour rose as her thoughts expanded. She nodded and managed to say, 'Okay!' Rebecca couldn't imagine why he cared about how she felt among his family or visitors, but it wasn't her job to question the ways of the rich and famous.

★   ★   ★

After lunch on Monday, Chiara knocked and entered with the two children in tow. Her curiosity about Rebecca had been growing ever since Marco mentioned Luca had known Rebecca a long time ago, and that he thought Luca was attracted. Chiara knew about Luca's various past girlfriends, but no one had lasted long. Usually, by the time the family was aware of someone new, the affair was almost over.

Antonia had been one of those short-lived episodes, and if she was typical of the kind of women Luca liked, Chiara wondered why Luca was attracted to Rebecca. Rebecca was undoubtedly pretty; she was also uncomplicated, had no allures, and treated everyone in the same down-to-earth manner. Chiara thought her refreshing because she was honest, outspoken, and didn't flatter. Luca's women were usually sophisticated, fussy, conceited — and sometimes arrogant. Chiara wondered if she should warn Rebecca about Luca, but decided not to. It was Marco's guesswork. If Luca did feel sexually attracted to a temporary secretary, it would burn itself out fast. Chiara still sympathised silently, but Rebecca was old enough to take care of herself.

'Hi, Rebecca, we've come to say goodbye. We're leaving soon.' She gave the two children a gentle push, and both of them shook hands politely. Chiara then let them off the hook and they disappeared. She sank into the nearest convenient chair.

'Whew! I like this place, but the

children run wild, and it's sometimes hard to keep them under control.'

Rebecca smiled. 'I bet we all tried to kick over the traces whenever we could, didn't we? Kids find their own limitations, and those of their parents!'

'Mmm! You're probably right. Why didn't you stay longer yesterday after the meal?'

'You know how I feel about butting in on family gatherings. I thought you'd all appreciate a little more privacy.'

'Your presence would have helped to calm the atmosphere. It was silly of my parents-in-law to give in and bring Antonia along. Perhaps they think Luca will reconsider, but I'm sure he won't. Even if Antonia's family and the Barsettis are close friends, no one should interfere.' She shifted in the chair, and watched Rebecca's expression as she continued to explain. 'Antonia grew up with Marco and Luca, and things were fine until Luca and Antonia had a brief affair. Now Luca turns into an iceberg whenever Antonia is around, and you could cut the atmosphere between them with a knife! Antonia still wants him, even though Luca moved on long ago.' Chiara studied her manicured nails, and then dragged her fingers through her hair.

Rebecca felt awkward listening to her. She didn't know the Barsetti family well, and she didn't want to comment. She didn't want to listen to tales about Antonia and Luca, either. It was all none of her business. She nodded vaguely, and hoped to distract Chiara when she asked, 'Where do you live?'

'Taranto; in one of the nicer areas, but it's still too loud, too polluted, and too overcrowded. I don't think you'd like it after this place, but I suppose beauty is in the eye of the beholder. One day, Marco and I will probably get round to moving to the outskirts; to a house like the one Luca has built for when he comes here for business. Taranto has always been company headquarters, and the men stick to tradition and are reluctant to move elsewhere. They prefer travelling the world than moving everything to a real top city. I love city life — the shops, entertainment, restaurants, cultural happenings. If you get the chance, come and visit me before you go back to London.' She reached for a piece of paper and a pencil. 'Here's our telephone number and address.'

Rebecca was surprised and pleased. 'I don't suppose I'll have the time, especially if there's another job waiting for me, but it's very kind of you, Chiara. Thanks!'

Chiara rose and shook the creases out of her bright turquoise skirt. On her way to the door, she turned with an afterthought. 'Oh, Grandma's looking forward to meeting you. So if you bump into an elderly lady somewhere on the premises, don't be surprised!'

Rebecca nodded. 'Have a safe journey.'

Chiara studied her watch. 'A helicopter is collecting us in half an hour. I'd better check the luggage. Bye!' Her skirt ballooned around the door as she left.

Rebecca wondered if Chiara was always so friendly to people she might never see again. She poured a fresh glass of cold water from the thermos jug and refocused her attention on work. She typed steadily, finished at the usual time, and thought longingly about a swim, but decided against it. The family might be on the beach. She had a shower instead, and settled on the terrace with a cool drink. The weakening sunlight edged through the foliage of nearby trees and made spotted golden patterns on the flagstones.

'Good afternoon! You must be Rebecca.'

Rebecca looked up into a pair of twinkling pale blue eyes. Their owner held herself erect like a post, but was leaning on a walking stick for support. Her silvery hair framed her face in a simple bob. She must have been a very beautiful woman in her youth. She was still handsome; the balanced proportions of her face were good, even though fine lines and wrinkles had reduced the former perfection.

'Yes. And if I'm not mistaken, you

must be Mrs Barsetti senior. Please!' She pulled a chair forward and patted the seat.

The old lady lowered herself slowly and rested the stick against the arm of the chair. A heavy gold bracelet tinkled as she arranged her skirt of her straw-coloured dress in tidy folds. She looked at Rebecca and smiled. 'I hope I'm not intruding, but I don't meet many English people these days. I enjoy talking to someone from home whenever I have the chance.'

'No, of course not! It's a pleasure! Would you like something to drink? Tea, perhaps? Franca gave me some of Luca's, so I can offer you a cup of real British tea.'

She looked approvingly at Rebecca's attractive face and friendly green eyes. 'That sounds lovely. If it's no trouble?'

'Back in a minute.'

Rebecca loaded the tray and added some digestive biscuits she'd brought with her. She arranged the crockery on the table, and sat down opposite her guest. Looking at the older woman's face, she decided that although age had taken some of her beauty, it had still left her with graceful elegance and personality. 'How long have you lived in Italy, Mrs Barsetti?'

'Oh, almost sixty years.'

'Sugar? Milk?'

'Just one spoonful of sugar, please.'

Rebecca poured the tea, and pushed the plate of biscuits nearer her guest. 'And do you still miss Britain?'

'It's all a lot easier these days — television, travel, and the internet. I still miss English humour, some typically English food, the smell of fresh-mown grass on a summer day . . . and I definitely miss the bookshops!' She laughed softly. 'Nowadays, that's improved, too. Luca showed me how to use the Internet for shopping, and I have a lot of fun searching for things and ordering what I want.'

'Are you ever homesick?'

'I used to miss family and my friends in the beginning, but so many of them are dead and gone now. No, I'm no longer homesick. I identified with Italy as soon as my son was born, and I've grown to love it very much. Today, I'm torn in two ways. I'm English inside, but I now belong to Italy.'

'What was the hardest part?'

It was quiet, and the sunlight was fading fast, but still found its way through the moving greenery, pouring splatters of yellow and copper across the flagstones at their feet. Mrs Barsetti looked into the distance; Rebecca could see she was thinking hard. 'The hardest part was being accepted. Italian families are very close units, and back then, things were even more difficult for an outsider in this part of Italy. If my husband hadn't supported me, been so determined and prepared to risk a family quarrel, I wouldn't be here today. It was a tough time for us both.'

Rebecca was intrigued. 'You never thought of going back home?'

The wrinkled hands with their age-spots were folded quietly in her lap, and she shook her head decisively. 'No! Leandro inherited two fishing boats from his father, gradually built a shipping empire, and then got involved in banking. He worked very, very hard, and I supported him all the way. He wouldn't have been happy in Britain; he loved the sunshine, the sea, and Italy. I love my homeland, but I loved Leandro more.'

'He must have been a very special man.'

'Wonderful! There's a photo in the living room; I'll show it to you next time you're in the house. He was very determined, ambitious, and clever, otherwise he wouldn't have succeeded so brilliantly. Those characteristics flowed over into our marriage, and we had an extraordinary life together. Our love was peppered by the clash of two stubborn personalities, so sometimes the sparks flew, but it was always fun.'

Rebecca took a sip of tea, and was absorbed. 'How long were you married?'

'Almost fifty-six years; he died four years ago. My son is fifty-nine; Marco is thirty-four, Luca is thirty-two. Luca has more of my husband in him than the others. He's my favourite, but please don't tell anyone I said so! I love them all, but Luca is so like Leandro. How do you like San Andrea? I hope Luca is a good boss?'

Rebecca avoided answering the later question, and replied, 'From what I've seen of the island, I'd say it's a wonderful combination of ancient and modern.'

'Yes, it is, isn't it? Sometimes I regret the way modern life has changed it, but . . .'

A rustle underfoot announced another visitor. Luca bent his head to duck under a tree and held a branch aside as his eyes took in the scene on the small patio. An arched eyebrow indicated surprise and humour, and his face lit up briefly when his eyes rested on his grandmother. 'There you are! We wondered where you were. Dad sent me to investigate. I've been to the beach on a wild goose chase, and across the field to the donkeys, I thought you might be there.'

Mrs Barsetti laughed. 'Serve you right. I know this island better than all of you. I spent a long time here until your grandfather and I moved to live on the mainland.'

'We were worried.'

'Were you? Why? I can take care of myself.'

He laughed. 'That's what I told Dad, but you know him.' He eyed the tea things. 'I see that you've found Rebecca. Reminiscing about England?' He turned to Rebecca; his eyes were still friendly and good-humoured. 'Gran is still British to the core; I'm always surprised at how Anglo-Saxon she is, even after all this time.'

'A leopard can't change its spots, Luca. Just remember: you're part-British, and you spend so much time there these days that you're more British than you realise.'

He laughed. 'I consider myself a European of Italian origin, with British overtones.'

'That's not a bad combination. What

do you think, Rebecca?'

She watched Rebecca looking at Luca with a faint flush on her cheeks. Rebecca was intelligent, modern, independent, and a pleasant girl. Her feet were planted firmly on the ground. Marco mentioned Luca and Rebecca had once known each other years ago; it was time Luca settled down! The old lady studied Luca's expression, and decided the situation was intriguing and full of promise.

'I don't think I'll comment; he's my boss, and he expects me to say something flattering, whether it's true or not!'

That evening, not many other women on earth could have competed with the crimson vision of Antonia's designer dress and elaborate hairstyle. In a moment of sheer silliness, Rebecca wished she'd worn the only other near-evening dress she'd brought with her, but she was wearing the white one again. Throwing back her shoulders and touching her hair reassuringly, she concentrated on getting through the evening, and reminded herself that

Antonia would always be the centre of attention wherever she went.

Even if they hoped Luca would return to Antonia, his parents were still polite and considerate to Rebecca. His father resembled Luca physically, although he was heavier, with bigger bones, and his hair was already grey. His mother was elegantly slim, and wore her clothes and jewellery with style. She was an effervescent personality. She noticed Rebecca's reticence to join in, and encouraged her. Antonia ignored Rebecca and eyed Luca constantly, although he didn't give her extra attention. Rebecca wished Chiara hadn't told her about Luca and Antonia. Antonia even started speaking Italian a couple of times, but Luca's grandmother cut her short. The three men spent most of the time talking business. Rebecca was glad that Luca's grandmother was there; it made all the difference.

She didn't join them in the sitting room when the meal ended. It was easy to forget that these people were rich. In a couple of weeks, she'd be working for someone else in a different place.

Next morning, she found a dictation tape waiting for her when she reached her office. The house might be full of visitors, but Luca didn't let that interfere with his work. She noticed he'd also picked up the finished pages from the previous day, and was no doubt already busy inserting corrections and making changes.

Now that she'd met everyone, she decided no one would mind if she went for a swim after work. It had been humid all day long, and the prospect was wonderful. She changed quickly, pulled a long T-shirt over her bikini, and grabbed a towel. She skipped lightly down the steps cut into the cliff, her anticipation growing, until the moment she saw Antonia and Luca coming up.

Antonia's skimpy bikini left nothing to the imagination, even if her figure was too skinny to be considered sexy. Luca moved with athletic ease. Together, they made a very attractive pair. Rebecca slowed her tempo, dawdling where one of the steps was wider so that they could pass with ease. Inexplicably, the prospect of a swim had lost some of its charm, and it got worse. When they drew level, she was expecting to exchange some inconsequential pleasantries, but Antonia cut her short.

'Oh, Miss . . . Miss?'

Rebecca tried not to show any irritation. 'Summer.'

Her voice was silken. 'Damn! I've left my sunglasses on the sunbed. Be a dear and fetch them?'

Bowled over by her cheek, Rebecca swallowed hard. 'No! They're your sunglasses. Fetch them yourself.'

Antonia's nostrils flared and she spluttered. 'How dare you! You're a paid employee!'

Rebecca was aware of Luca standing in the background, but that didn't stop her being as mad as a wet hen. She tried to regain some composure. 'Yes, I am — but I'm not *your* employee, Miss Lorenzo. I'm not paid to fetch your sunglasses, or anything else.' She continued on her way, and concentrating on not stumbling. Luca turned away casually to face the sea, but she heard a soft splutter. Antonia noticed too, and before Rebecca reached the beach, she heard Antonia's voice: 'Contemptible behaviour . . . Who does she think she is?'

Rebecca kept walking until she was at the edge of the sea. She threw down her towel and pulled her T-shirt over her head. She was shaking with anger and her breath was uneven. She took a deep breath and heard the sound of feet crunching on the pebbles further up the beach. Without looking, she knew it was Luca. Perhaps she was about to lose a lucrative job, but it was too late to worry about that now. She was not Antonia's housemaid. She looked steadily out to sea where a raft bobbed in the green water. She fled towards it.

5

Usually, she swam parallel to the shore, but now without thinking she aimed for the raft. She had to put distance between herself and the beach. She needed to get her anger under control before she could face Luca. She was still glad she hadn't given in. She realized Luca couldn't ignore the situation, but by the time they next met, her emotions would be under control again.

She swam as if the devil was on her heels. Her arms cut through the crystal waters cleanly, and every stroke brought her closer to her goal. She was conscious of Luca shouting, but she chose not to listen. Suddenly, Rebecca sensed that he was following her, and she tried to increase her speed. She wasn't very successful, and began to feel undercurrents that were making progress difficult. She'd almost reached the raft when he caught up. She turned her head and swallowed seawater; she coughed and submerged briefly. Resurfacing, she coughed even more, and fought to steady herself. He was close, treading water, and watching her. Seawater streamed down her face, and she felt hostile because he hadn't left her alone.

'Keep swimming!' His words were curt and pointed.

She figured she couldn't make it back without a rest anyway, so she shut her mouth and finished the distance. She grabbed a looped rope hanging on the side of the raft. Her chest was heaving with exertion. She didn't have the strength to pull herself up.

He hauled himself up easily and grabbed her arm. It ached as he pulled her from the water, but she didn't fuss. She wasn't going to be weak and complaining. She noticed how his lips thinned as he pulled her up, and suddenly remembered the broken ribs from the plane crash and was conscience-stricken. Rebecca was calmer now, and knew that she'd never have attempted to swim to the raft under normal circumstances. She was only an average swimmer, and she was out of practice. She bit her lip and avoided his eyes.

He squeezed the water out of his hair, and gazed at her. 'What got into you? Are you mad? I was scared that you'd get into trouble. The currents start to play havoc round here.'

She was still panting and trying to control her breathing. 'I know, you told me that once before! There's no reason for you to stay. You'd better go back. Miss Lorenzo is probably waiting.'

His lips curled in amusement. He lowered himself, propped his head on one arm, and looked at her. 'Antonia has scurried off in one hell of a temper.' He smiled and stared at her. She sensed a smouldering flame growing in his eyes.

Rebecca dragged her eyes away and sat down, lacing her hands around her knees. There was something danger-ously intimate about being alone with

Luca on a raft in the middle of a jade-coloured sea. She felt she ought to apologise — not to Antonia, to him. 'I'm sorry if I've caused trouble between you two, but I'm not her servant.' She drew a deep breath.

He moved his position slightly. He was more stunningly virile than ever; seawater was clinging in crystal drops to the dark hair on his chest. 'Forget it! I understand, perfectly. She often forgets herself; it's a by-product of all the attention she gets. She had no right to ask you to do anything for her, and when I told her so, that really ruffled her feathers!' He smiled broadly, and was then serious again when he continued, 'I was scared when I saw you running helter-skelter into the sea. I remembered you told me that you aren't the world's best swimmer.'

She nodded. For a while, they just sat in the sun. She brushed away trickles of seawater from her face with the back of her hand, and pushed some straggling strands of hair behind her ears. She must look awful.

There was a wistful look on her face, and they stared silently at each other. His gaze was riveted on her face, then moved over her body slowly. She ached for his touch, and the air around them was electric. He put his arm round her, pulling her to him, leaned forward and kissed her briefly. It was like a whisper on the breeze. His lips tasted salty and warm. She stiffened and then relaxed against him. She was shocked by her own eager response, how the pit of her stomach swirled as their bodies touched. His mouth curved lazily, and he pushed another straying tendril back behind her ear and kissed her more deeply again. Rebecca sensed that their kisses didn't just surprise her; they startled him, too.

She was totally confused. Eight years ago, she'd have given her soul for his kiss; now she wished it hadn't happened. She heard his quick intake of breath as he set her free.

She bent her head so that he couldn't see her face, and when she looked up at him, Rebecca still saw bewilderment. She could tell that he was analysing the situation. He pointed towards the beach. 'Shall we head back? Or do you need more time to recover?'

She shook her head wordlessly, and glided into the bluish-green water again. She was glad to escape. The water slid over her body like warm silk; the sea was calm, and she swam back slowly, aware that he was following. This time, she was glad to know he was there.

On the beach, her legs felt like rubber from the unaccustomed exercise. Water dripped from her body in rivulets. He picked up her towel and T-shirt, and handed them to her silently. He watched her closely as she dried herself. Rebecca tried not to stare as he took her towel to wipe himself too. She put on her T-shirt and waited until he finished rubbing his hair.

They walked silently side-by-side up the steps and back to the house. She was still breathless from the exertion of swimming — or was it from emotion? He made no attempt at conversation until they'd covered some ground. When they were about to branch off in different directions, he paused for a second and looked at her with an inscrutable expression.

'Promise that you'll never swim to the raft again unless someone else is around?'

She was perplexed by the tone of concern in his voice, and merely nodded silently.

'Good!'

Rebecca decided he was a mystery. She'd expected a reprimand, but he was on her side. She wanted to mention what happened on the raft, and say that they should avoid anything similar again . . . but she couldn't think of the right words, and also lacked the courage. She mused that it probably meant absolutely nothing to him. Perhaps it was sheer habit to flirt with any woman who crossed his path, given the chance.

'I'll see you at dinner.'

'Yes ... oh! I forgot. No! I'm meeting someone this evening.'

A hint of vexation hovered, but it faded quickly. He didn't ask any questions. 'Does Franca know?'

'Yes.'

He nodded briefly before turning away to go towards the house. Rebecca stood motionless for a while, staring at his departing figure. The setting sun covered his body in gold. She entertained a secret hope that he'd look back, but he didn't.

★ ★ ★

Later that evening, Rebecca was glad to get away. She'd have to face Antonia sometime, but not tonight. Antonia was too much of a star to ever act normally with Luca's temporary secretary. Silly woman! As if Rebecca presented any kind of danger to her plans to recapture Luca!

At least Luca hadn't dismissed her;

that was a consolation. It would have been disaster for the agency's reputation. She ignored the possibility that her reasons were more personal ones.

Peter was a gift from the gods that evening. He was solid, undemanding, and it was wonderful to forget fiery Italians for a while.

He picked her up and drove to a shoreline restaurant. When he handed her the menu, he said, 'This place has a reputation for the best clay-oven food on the island.'

She looked at the menu written in Italian and English and smiled. 'It's probably all good, but most of it sounds very exotic. I haven't a clue what to order.'

'Shall I choose? Something not too exotic?'

Rebecca nodded gratefully.

They ordered salad topped with goat's cheese, tender juicy lamb with young vegetables, and finished a delicious meal with coffee and squares of puff pastry filled with ground almonds and coated with syrup and honey.

Rebecca patted her mouth with her serviette and leaned back contentedly. 'That was wonderful. I love Italian food.'

He laughed. 'It is usually very good, isn't it?'

She looked around the busy restaurant and towards setting sun. The sky was plastered in brilliant reds, oranges and yellows, and the sea mirrored the colours. 'This is a nice place. Did someone recommend it to you?'

'Yes, someone staying at my hotel. There are a couple of good eating-places on the island. Have you seen the ruins of the castle yet? There's a small restaurant nearby that's supposed to be excellent.'

'No. I don't have much free time, and no transport. Is it worth visiting?'

'A must! I went there yesterday. It's in all the tourist guides. Island inhabitants still believe there's a ghost who appears regularly. I didn't see it.'

Rebecca laughed.

He nodded, and indicated towards the small crowd on the dance floor. 'Italians love celebrating, and they also love music and dance.' The small live band was playing a repertoire of folk music and popular hits.

She twirled the stem of her glass, and watched the liquid settling again. 'We British are very conventional, aren't we? Can you imagine someone dancing or singing at the top of their voices in a local British pub?'

He laughed. 'Well, not really, but if someone chinks too much . . . times are changing!'

'Hello, Rebecca!'

Luca's voice made her jump. Some of the contents of her glass of wine spilled over her fingers.

'What a waste!' Luca watched as Rebecca wiped her fingers with her serviette.

Tilting her head to look up at him, Rebecca was at a loss for words. Next to him, Antonia was waiting impatiently to move on. She ignored Rebecca and remained silent.

Rebecca managed to sound calm. 'Hello!' Luca made no attempt to move on, so she was obliged to make introductions. 'This is Peter Stanley.' Luca held out his hand. 'Peter, this is my boss, Mr Luca Barsetti, and Miss Antonia Lorenzo.'

Peter got up to shake hands. Rebecca thought he'd already recognised Antonia. Perhaps Luca's name wasn't so well-known, but the fact that he was Rebecca's employer was enough. He was impressed.

Luca indicated towards the empty chairs with his long fingers. 'May we join you? Or are we interrupting something?'

Rebecca's mouth fell open and she glared, but Peter said politely, 'By all means.'

Antonia was visibly annoyed, but Luca was already waiting with her chair. She slid gracefully into it and took cigarettes and a lighter out of her bag. She was wearing a cream slub-silk dress, and a matching scarf was slung loosely round her neck. Peter hurried to proffer a lighter for her cigarette.

'No one minds, I hope?' Without waiting for a reply, she blew a column of blue smoke into the air, and leaned back with practiced boredom. Rebecca noticed that she'd caught the attention of other guests at nearby tables who immediately recognised her.

Rebecca wished they'd gone somewhere else. If someone came to the table to ask Antonia for an autograph, she'd be tempted to scream! This was supposed to be *her* evening out with Peter, but Luca had pitched them centre-stage. Lively music was still playing in the background, and the blue and red lampions hanging from the posts at the edge of the terrace moved lazily in the evening breeze. Rebecca looked at them and then at Luca. She avoided looking at Antonia, and heard Luca asking Peter what he did for a living. Rebecca leaned back, sipped on her glass, and gazed out to sea. After this afternoon, there was no reason for her to be pleasant to Antonia. She pretended to be spellbound by the fading sunset.

'Luca, I want to dance.' Antonia's sensual voice drifted lethargically across the table. The men were talking about the Italian resistance movement during the Second World War.

'Do you? I'm sure Peter would love to dance, wouldn't you, Peter?'

Peter was put on the spot, but was too polite to refuse. 'My pleasure.' The tall Englishman stood up.

Antonia didn't like Luca's evasion tactics, but she was clever enough not to make a scene, and gave in without a comment. She ground out the tip of her cigarette, got up, and tucked her arm through Peter's.

Rebecca watched them make their way to the small dance floor. They matched in height, and Peter was a good dancer. In the spotlight, where she felt at home, Antonia looked almost content as they glided around.

Rebecca caught Luca's eye as her glance drifted back to their table. She looked away quickly, and made imaginary patterns on the tablecloth with her fingertip.

He raised a dark, slightly sardonic eyebrow. 'Mad?'

'Mad?' She glanced at him with an innocent expression, but couldn't hide the irritation in her voice. 'Whatever makes you think that?'

He smiled knowingly. 'Oh, just a hunch. Am I butting in on something serious?'

She replied rather stiffly, 'I only met Peter the other day. He invited me for a meal this evening.' Once she'd explained, she wondered why she'd done so. It wasn't Luca's business what she did.

'You met him here?'

'Yes.' She crossed her arms across her chest in a defensive gesture and looked across the terrace before she stared back at him determinedly again. 'Not that it's any of your business.'

'No.' There was a trace of laughter in his voice. 'I'll shut my mouth, and we'll both study the sunset.'

Against all her better judgement, she spluttered and had to laugh; he was too pleasing. Did he affect all women in the same way? Despite the fact that his presence produced collywobbles somewhere between her heart and her head, she also felt something exciting was happening. She ignored the thought that history was merely repeating itself. She waited.

'Okay . . . I know I shouldn't have intruded, but you were a godsend. Antonia was determined to go out this evening, and so I'd two alternatives: either take her out, or put up with her sulks for the rest of the day. That would have meant a very depressing evening for my parents and my grandmother.'

She paused, raised her eyebrows, and tried to sound bland. 'So you sacrificed yourself? That's very commendable!' She sighed and looked at him. 'I suppose there's no harm done — although my private life is my own affair, even on San Andrea.'

'Okay! I'll make up it up to you one day. Let's dance.'

'What?'

'Let's dance.' He reached out and skimmed the surface of her arm with his fingers.

Her senses were already in turmoil and signalling warnings to her brain before he'd touched her. When he grabbed her hand, the result was electrical shocks. It was too late to think of an excuse. With her hand in his, he pulled her to her feet. She was startled, but managed to forget her confusion long enough to say, 'Antonia will be as mad as a bluebottle! You practically threw her at Peter. She wanted you to dance with her.'

He shrugged. 'I wish you wouldn't question my decisions all the time, Rebecca.'

In his arms on the small dance floor, the top of her head reached his shoulder. He pulled her close. She leaned against him, and tried to ignore the hardness of his body and her own reaction. One hand rested on her bare back; it felt warm and possessive and wakened erotic feelings. Rebecca wished she hadn't chosen to wear this particular dress tonight; the neckline was demure in the front, but plunged more generously in the back. Vaguely, she registered that people around them were singing along to a raucous-sounding song, but for a moment or two she continued to drift along in her own world. She allowed her emotions to take over, despite her intention to keep him at arm's length. In his arms, she could only think what an exceptional man he was. She shouldn't ask herself if he was a good lover, but the physical effect he had on her spoke volumes! She stared, slightly mesmerized by the closeness of his face, and inhaled the invisible cloud of musky male fragrance that surrounded him as they moved in unison. She needed to break the spell. 'People seem to like this, what do the words mean?'

His voice caressed her hair. 'It's a super-schmaltzy love song, and it's all the rage at the moment. Don't ask me to translate — I refuse outright!'

'It sounds fun.' She swallowed hard and listened to the loud and happy rendition, without understanding a word; it helped to direct her thoughts in another direction — away from him.

Rebecca wouldn't have been so unconcerned if she'd noticed how carefully people were watching them. People exchanged knowing smiles and nudges. The Barsetti family was well-known. Marco and Luca spent a lot of their leisure time on the island.

Luca thought about how much Rebecca interested him. She'd been a good friend eight years ago, and they'd got on extremely well, despite their different backgrounds and points of view. He was surprised how he still enjoyed talking to her, and how he just liked being with her. She was confident, with a strength of character that did not lessen her femininity — perhaps they were the same qualities that had attracted him when he was a student.

He could relax and be himself with her. Things were different now, though. This afternoon on the raft had made that clear. There was chemistry at work. She attracted him physically as well as mentally. The music ended, and she immediately withdrew from his arms; suddenly, they felt very empty.

When they returned to the table, Antonia and Peter were already seated. Antonia was puffing away again on a thin-stemmed cigarette. Her beautiful eyes were narrow slits of silent disapproval as she watched them. Rebecca wondered why someone blessed with such beauty wasn't more relaxed. If she wanted Luca, she wouldn't get him by browbeating him, making him feel guilty, or showing open disapproval.

They sat down. Luca loosened his tie and asked, 'Wine? Ouzo?'

Antonia studied her watch. 'No! Let's go, Luca!' Another half-finished lipstick-smeared cigarette landed in the overflowing ashtray.

He smothered her comment. 'Peter

hasn't finished his drink, I haven't started mine, and Rebecca wants another glass of wine.' Rebecca blinked, but didn't protest. 'Anyway, what's the hurry all of a sudden? You couldn't wait to get out an hour ago!'

She laughed weakly. 'No hurry, darling! I just thought you might be tired.'

He eyed her coldly. 'Well, I'm not.' He turned to Peter. 'Where else have you been in Italy, Peter?'

Antonia pretended to show interest for a while, but soon made no effort to hide her boredom when she failed to attract Luca's attention. Both women were silent. Antonia found waiting tedious, and Rebecca didn't contribute to the conversation. She wasn't well versed in the lives of Roman philosophers. Unheeding the atmosphere, or just not caring, Luca carried on a two-way conversation with Peter. It was Peter who eventually noted Antonia's boredom. Politely, he said, 'The women are bored. Perhaps we should call it a day?'

Luca eyed Antonia with vexation,

looked at his watch, and shrugged. 'I suppose so. But there's no need for you to take Rebecca home, Peter. She can come with us.' His voice was dogmatic, and Rebecca considered rebelling, but decided it would be childish. She didn't like scenes if she could avoid them.

Peter didn't seem to mind very much. 'Perhaps we can meet again, Rebecca — before I leave?'

Giving Rebecca no chance to reply, Luca asked, 'When will that be?'

'End of the week.'

'You must come up to the house for a meal one evening before you leave.'

Rebecca felt as if she was in limbo: someone else was talking for her and making all the decisions. She tried to hide her irritation.

'Where are you staying?' Luca continued.

'With a family named Pignatelli down near the harbour.'

'They have a small hotel and a restaurant?'

'That's right.'

He nodded. 'I know them. I'll phone you, and arrange something as soon as it's more peaceful up at the house. Ready, Antonia? Rebecca?'

Antonia was already gliding towards Luca's car. Typically impolite and uncouth, she didn't even say goodnight to Peter.

Rebecca turned to him. 'Thanks for a lovely meal, Peter; I enjoyed it.' That was the truth. It had been pleasant, until the other two turned up. 'We'll see each other soon?'

Peter bent and kissed her chastely on the cheek. 'Yes!' He straightened and stuck his hand out. 'Goodbye, Luca.'

'Not goodbye . . . goodnight! I'll be in touch!' He shook Peter's hand and gave him a reassuring pat on the shoulder before he slid his hand under Rebecca's elbow. She made an unspectacular but determined effort, and freed herself before they reached the car.

6

Antonia got in the front. Rebecca slid into the back seat when Luca opened the door. The journey was a silent one. Looking out of the window, Rebecca noticed there was a half-moon, edged with bright silver, and the stars burned bright in a clear velvet sky. The road twisted and scrambled through the darkness, and the headlights cut through the gloom like a knife. Music from the radio played softly in the background. There was little traffic at this time of the night.

In a matter of minutes, the car reached the turn-off to its final destination. The headlights lit up the stonework wall surrounding the property for a brief moment, before they drove down the track and finally came to stop in front of the house.

Antonia remained where she was, hoping for a helping hand that didn't materialise. She finally placed her long legs on the ground outside, and rose elegantly to her feet. Rebecca got out and slammed the door. His eyebrows lifted, his mouth twitched, and he turned to Antonia.

'You can go in. I'll take Rebecca across to the outhouse.'

Antonia said something in Italian and traipsed off towards the entrance door.

'I don't need your . . . ' Rebecca got no further. With his hand firmly under her elbow, he steered her towards the outhouse. She fell into step, silent until they were out of earshot, then hissed, 'Stop using me as a shock absorber. Why don't you just sort things out properly with Antonia? She blames me for what's wrong between you and her. If she could, she'd axe me.'

He threw back his head and laughed; it echoed through the silence around them. His eyes sparkled in the darkness. 'You enjoy telling me what I should do, don't you? A showdown with Antonia would be a volcanic eruption. She'd wake everyone in a radius of five miles.

Rebecca, I'm not avoiding Antonia. She knows it's over, she just won't accept it. I don't intend to waste my energy in arguing with her all the time. We're finished, and that's that!'

Their feet crunched on the gravel as they neared the outhouse. She'd already asked herself if it was always wise to say what she was thinking, but the temptation was too great.

'She still believes she has certain rights . . . not that it's any of my business, of course.'

He answered, 'At the time, the tableau press had a heyday, and it certainly made interesting reading, I didn't recognise myself most of the time. Antonia doesn't accept that it was a wrong move for both of us, but she'll have to.' They halted in front of the door. 'So, here you are. Home again! Lock your door! Remember, the island tradition says we have a monster who appears from time to time looking for a victim!'

'What?' Her voice echoed in the

darkness. 'Now you really are being ridiculous!'

'Apparently, it fancies a young woman for breakfast now and then. Ask Giraldo, or anyone else who lives here! We have our own monster!'

'Stop joking! I don't believe you for a second. Are you referring to the male kind, on two legs, with dark hair and dark eyes?'

His voice was full of laughter. 'Who knows? Night, Rebecca!'

Without replying, she marched into the outhouse and shut the door with an audible thud. She heard the faint sound of his steps on the loose gravel as he walked away. He whistled softly, and it carried to her on the breeze. She resisted the urge to watch him through the window. He'd ruined her evening with Peter, and used them both — just to keep Antonia happy.

It took Rebecca a while to fall asleep; the picture of Antonia in Luca's arms kept her awake. He'd more or less admitted that they'd been lovers; the idea bothered her much too much. She realized she was growing increasingly vulnerable to his charm, and she knew she had to break free or she'd suffer. If he noticed she liked him, he'd take advantage and then cast her aside. According to the newspapers, that was how he always treated his girlfriends.

She was already at work when he appeared next morning, and to her annoyance, she felt herself immediately responding to him despite all her determination to be impervious. He lit excitement in her soul. She felt like the student girl of eight years ago — breathless, a little confused, apprehensive, and on tenterhooks whenever he was near.

'Morning, Rebecca! Everything okay? Any questions? Here's the next bit of dictation. Here are chapters seven, eight and nine back — all okay.'

His handsome bronzed forehead creased in lines of concentration as he sorted the papers into various piles. She mused that it wasn't fair that he was so good-looking when wealth and standing had been his from birth anyway. She struggled to find a casual tone and held out her hand. 'Thanks.' Just the way he stood there, in his casually expensive clothes, told you he'd made it. Sometimes Rebecca wished she could rock his composure a little, just enough to bewilder him in the way he bewildered her.

'Antonia has to leave today for a photo shooting. Thank heavens! Our evening meal won't be fraught with negative vibrations.' He expected no comment and got none. He was already at the door, and turned and touched his forehead in a mock salute. He was so infuriatingly sexy she wanted to throw something heavy at him in frustration.

She was glad Antonia was missing when she went for the evening meal. She avoided looking at Luca and the conversation was general, mostly about current political happenings in Italy, so she couldn't contribute much. Luca seemed preoccupied with his own thoughts. Perhaps he liked Antonia more than he realized? Rebecca knew he could easily disguise his real feelings. He could listen closely, and plan something completely different at the same time. She guessed he was a ruthless businessman, but the other side of his character showed her that he cared a great deal about his family. What did it matter what she thought? Luca would forget her existence before the ferry left the jetty.

She relaxed and concentrated on the conversation. His mother asked her about the agency, where she lived in London, about her parents, and seemed genuinely interested. Luca's father asked about her father's small building company. Rebecca had no idea what her father was doing at the moment, and said so. 'I'm busy in the agency all the time. I don't have time to keep up with what Dad is doing in his business.'

Luca's mother remarked, 'I wish I'd had the chances young women have today, when I was young.'

Luca's father added hurriedly, 'I'm

glad you didn't. I'd have had the devil's own trouble to catch you if you'd been a career-woman! I had enough trouble as it was.' She chuckled.

Rebecca's intention to leave as soon as the meal finished was thwarted when Luca's grandmother asked her to play dominos. The next hour was a pleasant change from her solo evenings in the outhouse. Luca was reading in a winged chair in a corner of the living room, and his parents were watching television in the adjoining room.

'I've won twice, and you once. Another game? I haven't played for ages. I used to play it a lot with my grandsons, didn't I, Luca?' His murmured assent was lost in the depths of the room. 'It's such an easy game, isn't it?'

'Mmm! I often used to play with my grandfather. He usually won.'

'Is he still alive?'

'No, he died two years ago. He was a love; I miss him.'

Mrs Barsetti was shuffling the stones

for the next game. 'I'm having a social evening to collect some funds for our orphanage. Will you come, Rebecca?'

'An orphanage?'

'The company has supported it for many years. Some of the children who were there in the beginning are now adults. You must come.'

She was lost for words, but Mrs Barsetti didn't wait for an answer. 'Good!' She addressed her grandson: 'Luca! Bring Rebecca with you?'

His voice sounded brusque. 'If Rebecca wants to come, naturally.'

Rebecca wondered if he disapproved. She felt awkward. 'It's very kind, Mrs Barsetti, but my agency can't afford more than a small contribution . . . '

'Heavens, child! I'm not asking you because of money, I just thought you might like to meet some other people while you're here. No ifs or buts! Come! You'll need to stay overnight, so bring your things. You can stay with me.'

Overnight? Luca wouldn't approve of

125

his grandmother putting her up. 'I . . . I . . .'

The subject was closed; Mrs Barsetti was examining her dominoes. 'Aha! A good selection; I'm on a winning streak again.'

Rebecca checked her own. 'Don't be so sure about that!'

Half an hour later, Rebecca looked at her watch and stood up. She smiled at his grandmother, and saw kindness and approval there. 'Goodnight, Mrs Barsetti!'

'Goodnight. Rebecca.'

Luca was silent, and didn't look up when she called 'Goodnight,' although his parents echoed her farewell. Perhaps he hadn't heard her?

His grandmother watched Luca's face carefully as he followed Rebecca with his eyes as she left. She'd had a hunch about Rebecca from the start, and was beginning to believe it was more than just a hunch. Was history going to repeat itself?

A day or two later, Luca's parents

and grandmother left for the mainland again. The house seemed quiet with just the two of them at the dining table. Rebecca felt nervous now they were alone again, and wondered if the tension she felt was just her own imagination.

Working hours were always professional, and they stuck to generalities. In the evening, Luca didn't talk much about the recent visitors, and Antonia's name didn't crop up in their conversation either. Rebecca wondered if he was trying to avoid too much familiarity now they were alone again. She told herself that she was glad if he did.

When she was finishing the day's typing on Wednesday, he surprised her. 'I phoned Peter and invited him to come this evening.'

'That was kind of you.'

His expression was bland. 'You know I always keep my promises.'

She displayed an ease that she didn't feel. 'I only mean that I imagine you need to be wary about meeting strangers who might want to take advantage. You didn't need to invite Peter after such a fleeting acquaintance.'

'I spoiled your evening with him.' She didn't reply, so he continued, 'It's the least I can do.' He stood motionless in front of her desk and studied her with enigmatic dark eyes.

She swallowed hard, and was anxious to escape from his scrutiny. As long as things were professional, it was easy to ignore her feelings. It was only when her thoughts began to gallop along at an uncontrolled speed that very unprofessional thoughts emerged. She had an urge to touch him. She picked up a pile of typed sheets and got up too quickly; the papers fell in a cream fan across the desk. As she bent forward to gather them, he did too. Their fingers touched and their eyes met. She felt a shock run through her before he straightened up quickly and went towards the door.

'See you later.'

The door closed quietly, and Rebecca

stared at it, her heart pounding too fast. Her stomach whirled and she knew it was useless to pretend he didn't attract her. He radiated a vitality and virility that she was powerless to resist. He always had. She recalled the talks, the laughter, the companionship all those years ago, the kiss on the raft the other day, and how wonderful it had felt recently in his arms as they danced. The chemistry and the sensual attraction were there; nothing had changed.

She hurried to clear her desk for the day, and concentrated on the evening ahead. She told herself she was genuinely looking forward to seeing Peter again. Even if Luca had charisma, Peter was the kind of man she should choose to spend her life with. Peter was dependable, trustworthy, and faithful. Luca and she belonged to different worlds. If she offered herself to him, he'd take her. Why not? She'd be an amusing adventure with a little secretary. She'd satisfy his sexual appetite, boost his ego, and then he'd drop her like a hot potato.

The evening was a success. Peter seemed to enjoy himself. Luca was a practised and good host. Franca's cooking skills provided a memorable meal. It included some delicious chick-pea stew that was an island speciality. One day, when this job was over, she'd look back on this particular evening with almost undivided pleasure. After the meal, it was pleasant to lean back in a comfortable armchair and let her mind drift along, or join in with the two men's conversation. It also gave her some time to watch Luca's face and study his gestures, something she usually avoided.

When it was time to leave, he accompanied them to Peter's hired car. The moon was silver and brilliantly bright. The night air was balmy, full of the scent of the sea and the sharp perfume of juniper and cypresses.

She leaned forward to kiss Peter briefly on his cheek. 'Bye, Peter! I hope we'll meet again.'

There was no doubt in the sincerity of his voice. 'I hope so, too.' They'd already exchanged home addresses. 'I'll contact you the next time I'm in London? Perhaps we could go to the theatre, or a concert?'

'Mmm!' Rebecca tried mentally to dismiss the silent, motionless figure standing at her side. 'Do! I'd like that.'

Peter folded his lanky figure into the confinements of the small car. The headlights lit up whitewashed walls; her eyes followed the tail-lights until they disappeared from sight. She almost forgot Luca's presence. She was busy thinking if she really wanted to see Peter again in the future. Yes . . . he was nice.

Luca's voice forced its way in on her reflections. 'Would you like a nightcap?' His face was partially hidden in the shadows.

'No, thanks!' She turned towards the outhouse, and he fell into step beside her. 'It was an enjoyable evening, but all good things come to an end.'

He paused. His eyes glittered in the pale light of the moon; his voice sounded rough. 'It depends if you want them to end, or not.'

Rebecca didn't want to analyse his words. She was genuinely tired. 'Goodnight, Luca! I think Peter enjoyed himself.' She paused. 'Me too, of course.'

'Your thanks are enough.' The seductive tone of his voice (or was it a sudden cool breeze blowing in from the sea?) sent goose-pimples rippling across her skin. She reasoned that he knew every trick in the book about how to awaken desire in women; it was probably second nature to him by now.

'I like your Peter, he's an intelligent chap.'

'I agree; he is nice, and he is intelligent, but he's not mine. I met him here, remember? I'll probably never see him again.'

Now his voice was heavy with cynicism. 'Oh, come off it! He's on the edge of your web — attracted, losing orientation, and waiting for you to give him a sign. Women are all the same!'

She blinked in the darkness. 'What on earth are you talking about?' She tried to smother her anger. 'If you've burnt your own fingers too often, I suggest you try harder to avoid the flames. Don't worry about Peter Stanley's fate — he's too decent to attract the wrong kind of woman.'

He stood in the darkness, his eyes hidden by the dark, hands in his pockets. 'I'm not worrying about his fate; I'm worrying about my own.'

'Don't — you don't need to . . . the devil looks after his own.' She bit her lip in vexation. She was too tired; she didn't like baiting him. He was silent, and to her surprise, he didn't answer. Before she turned away, she added a hurried, 'Goodnight!'

His voice had a tinge of irony. 'Goodnight, Rebecca!'

She was glad to turn away, and forced herself not to check to see if he was still standing there, or on his way back to the house. Inside, she leaned her shoulders against the smooth surface of the whitewashed walls and closed her eyes. Her long, dark lashes fanned across her pale skin.

Much later, thumping her pillow, she hated herself for losing too much sleep over Luca Barsetti.

A short distance away, Luca took a small glass of whisky out onto the terrace and loosened his tie. He hitched himself onto the balustrade and stared out into the darkness. He was finding it harder and harder to be indifferent. It was a new experience for him; usually it was easy to be logical when a woman was involved. Rebecca was a friend from the past, who happened to be working for him at present. He still hadn't figured out what had driven him to kiss her on the raft, and he'd deliberately avoided thinking about it. To be honest he was also relieved that she hadn't mentioned it later. If she'd asked for an explanation, he would have had to admit he didn't have one. On top of that, this evening he was bothered because he found that he didn't enjoy sharing Rebecca with Peter. He wasn't jealous, he knew Rebecca too well for that — didn't he? He swallowed the liquid in one hasty gulp and made his way indoors again, his thoughts still turning in circles.

7

He was late coming to the office next morning.

'I'm off to the mainland, to an urgent board meeting of one of the subsidiary companies, and for an appointment with the skin specialist about this.' He waved his bandaged hand in the air. 'I'll continue dictating till I go. You can pick it up from the living room when you're ready.'

Rebecca looked up at him in surprise, and nodded silently. His dark eyes held hers, and she searched around in vain for a suitable comment, but his voice went on before her thoughts had caught up.

'You have enough to keep you busy until Tuesday or Wednesday?'

She cleared her throat. That was four or five days away; suddenly she couldn't imagine not seeing him until then. 'Yes.

I still have lots to do.'

He gave her the hint of a smile, and Rebecca felt her breath cut off for a moment. His puzzling attitude of last night was forgotten in a single glance.

He said, 'If you run out of work, take time off; we're on schedule. But remember what I said about swimming out too far.'

She thought about his fear of flying, and asked, 'Are . . . are you going by helicopter?'

'No. By catamaran.' His lips suddenly stretched to a thin line, and the creases around his mouth deepened. His mouth clenched tighter. 'I still have my problems about being above the clouds.'

'Understandable.'

Talking as much to himself as to Rebecca, he said, 'I'll have to get over it. It's essential. In the long run, my life won't function unless I can fly.'

She cleared her throat and hoped she sounded matter-of-fact. 'You can always use digital technology, or make your business partners come to you instead of the other way round, until you can. There's no point in pushing yourself beyond your limits.'

She should have known better than to show sympathy. His expression was grim. 'That's not how you run a business. It might work for a very short time, but not for long. I need my customers, not the other way round. In any case, it's my problem, not yours.'

She was glad she was sitting with her back to the window, so that he couldn't see how the colour rose in her face. Her breath quickened, and she turned back to the keyboard for want of something to do.

He watched her for a moment, and suddenly the harshness left his face and he made a weak attempt at apology. 'Listening to other people's sympathetic suggestions doesn't come easily. I'm sure you mean well.'

She leaned back, her fingers in her lap, and laughed shakily before she ploughed on. 'I'm positive that anyone who was in a plane crash, and came out of it alive, will never forget it. Be grateful that you're still alive. Things will improve, and I'm sure that you will fly again one day without fear.'

He was silent, and walked towards the window. 'Let's hope so!' He looked at his wristwatch; a shaft of sunlight caught the metal frame, and it flashed at her briefly before he turned away. 'I'd better get as much dictation as I can finished before I leave.' Moving towards the door, he looked back hastily over his shoulder, and gave her a weak smile. 'You're welcome to borrow my car if you want to explore one day. I'll tell Giraldo.'

Rebecca stared for a couple of seconds at the closed door. She was flummoxed by his generosity. Sometimes he set her teeth on edge, sometimes she longed to be with him all the time, and sometimes he bewildered her. Her emotions were seesawing out of control. Despite all the good intentions she'd had to shake off the past, it hadn't worked so far. The opposite was happening: his physical nearness made her senses spin, and now more than ever, she couldn't imagine wanting to spend her life with any other man.

She stood back from the office window, so that he wouldn't see her, and watched as Giraldo drove him to the port.

She kept to working hours and got through tasks more smoothly than usual; probably because there was no one there to interrupt the flow. Her thoughts flew across the green waters and she wondered where he was, what he was doing.

No one in the family was scheduled to visit the house, so Franca and Giraldo had permission to visit some relatives on the mainland if Rebecca agreed. She did. She was quite capable of managing alone. Giraldo gave her a lesson in handling Luca's car, and handed her the keys of the house and their telephone number in case of an emergency. Their luggage bounced madly as Giraldo cut corners on the track to the road. Franca's loud protests drifted back while Rebecca watched indulgently.

Alone at last, she loved the feeling of the soft winds hugging the building as they swept inland from the ocean. There wasn't much likelihood that anyone, apart from the goats or the donkeys, would stray to the house, but she was always careful about locking doors, especially at night.

After the luxury of a lengthy breakfast next day, she decided to do a little exploring. Before she set out, she studied a tourist brochure she'd picked up. She reversed Luca's car out of the garage and set off when it was still cool. Careful at first, until she'd accustomed herself to the powerful engine, she drove until a road sign pointed her in the right direction to one of the old towns. Once she was there, Rebecca understood why people fell in love with Italy, and decided it had something to do with the merging of ancient history and modern living.

The town wasn't often targeted by tourists, and she parked on the outskirts. After wandering for a while, she found a simple bodega and enjoyed a cool drink beneath a leafy pergola. Studying the locals, she noted that old men gathered to gossip with friends at the roadsides. Local women and younger men were always busy with their various tasks.

That evening, she phoned her business partner.

'Rebecca! How's it going?'

'Great. And you?'

'I'm fine. There's a new customer in the offing. An accounting company made some tentative enquiries last week. Oh, and that firm of solicitors you worked for last year asked if you'll be available in September. I said you'd be in touch.'

'That sounds encouraging; email me their address and number. I'll contact them as soon as I know when this job is finishing.'

'I miss our gossip sessions!'

'So do I! You've posted off that book I wanted? The one for Mrs Barsetti?'

'Yes. I sent it by express delivery. It'll get there any day now. I'm bursting with curiosity about your visit. From what I've read about him, you should watch your step with Luca Barsetti — even if you met him years ago. Be careful!'

Rebecca forced a laugh, ignoring the lump in her throat. She mused that it was already too late for warnings about Luca.

She worked steadily through Monday. Giraldo and Franca came back on Tuesday. When Luca didn't return on Wednesday morning, her disappointment was almost tangible. By the afternoon, she tried to forget him by rechecking the work they'd finished. She jumped when the phone rang; it was Giraldo.

'It's Luca. I'll put him through, hold the line.'

She held her breath and waited with her pulse accelerating.

'Rebecca?' His voice sent a ripple of awareness through her. She thought briefly about the sensible woman with her intentions to never get emotionally involved with an employer — especially this one. He repeated, 'Rebecca?'

She floundered, and to her dismay, her voice broke slightly. 'Yes. Hello!'

'I'm not returning. It's not worth coming back for one day, so I'll invest the time to clear up some loose ends here.'

She found her voice again, and mumbled, 'Okay.'

'Is everything alright?'

She took a deep breath. To her relief, her voice sounded fine again. 'Yes. I've caught up with the dictation. The publisher has sent some queries. If I can't solve them, they'll have to wait till you get back. Oh, how's — how's your hand?'

'My hand? Oh, it's fine. The doctor was satisfied, and I don't need bandages any more. It's healed well.'

Rebecca pictured how small lines

formed between his brows when he concentrated and his smile. She realized she wasn't listening properly when he uttered: ' . . . so, take the catamaran on Friday; I'll get Giraldo to book. The ferry wouldn't get you here on time for you to relax before the get-together. I'll meet you.'

She hurried to protest. 'That's not necessary. I'll find my own way. I've got her address. I'm used to taking care of myself.'

His voice was impatient. 'I'm sure you are, but I'll decide if I'll be there or not.' There was a slight pause. 'Tell Giraldo to send me the arrival time.' He sounded satisfied. He was making the decisions again.

She couldn't argue; he was her boss. Rebecca didn't like others arranging her schedule, and was glad that he couldn't see her face. She ought to be flattered that he was prepared to sacrifice his time. He could have just sent a car. She knew from her own experience that it was often better to have a car or booked taxi waiting for you at the ferry. Any for-hire taxis were usually snapped up by the first people off the boat. It still didn't mean it was necessary for him to come personally. She shrugged and kept quiet.

The crossing was a little bumpy, but it was faster and more expensive. She'd had no say in the arrangements, so she didn't waste time thinking about the cost. The metal hull skimmed the green waves, leaving a trail of frothy water as it headed for the mainland.

On arrival, the turmoil on the quay faded away when her eyes focused on Luca, leaning against the bonnet of a long, sleek limousine parked alongside one of the harbour warehouses. He looked at ease with himself, and extremely elegant in a lightweight grey business suit and conservative blue tie. For a second, Rebecca relished the thought that he was waiting for her. He lifted his hand when he saw her, and she waved back. She calmed her breathing and steadied her heartbeat as she left the ship and went towards him.

His eyes sparkled when they viewed her. He gave her a crooked smile and she couldn't stop herself smiling back. Her red-and-white skirt swirled around her legs as the warm winds played with the flimsy material; the white silk top skimmed her breasts and merged neatly with the skirt at the narrow belted waist.

'Had a good journey?'

'Yes, thanks. Hope you haven't been waiting long?'

'No more than necessary! Let me take that.'

Her own suitcase was too large for a short stay, so she'd borrowed a battered holdall from Franca. Their hands brushed briefly, and her colour heightened, but he'd already turned away to hand the bag to the waiting chauffeur. Rebecca was glad for the chance to cover her confusion. It was getting harder to remain coherent when he was near her.

He opened the door of the car and she slid inside. The cool air-conditioning was refreshing after the muggy heat on the quayside. Rebecca leaned back in a corner. He got in, closing the door with a thud. Opening his jacket, he leaned back into the soft leather upholstery and folded his long legs. His arm was resting leisurely along the back of the seat. The engine purred smoothly and Rebecca noticed the chauffeur was sizing her up in the mirror. Luca nodded at him and they set off.

She looked out of the window to avoid his gaze.

'So, how are you?'

All her efforts to remain calm were pointless. He made her feel legless, and her pulse was completely haywire. Her cheeks had pink spots. 'Me? I'm fine. You too, I hope?'

His eyes roamed over her reclining figure. 'Never felt better.'

Rebecca detected laughter in his eyes. She folded her hands for want of something better to do, and faced him defiantly. 'That's good. I didn't know if you'd want to see the publisher's queries.

I've brought them with me.'

There was dry amusement in his voice. 'Have you? Let's forget work for a while.'

Rebecca glanced out of the side window as the car sped through suburbs. She didn't ask where they were; it was pointless. She'd never come here again. 'How's your grandmother? Is she nervous?'

'Oh, she's fine. She enjoys these affairs. She's involved herself in this orphanage as long as I can remember. A dinner party gives her the chance to see people she likes, and collect money for a good cause.' He paused. 'She likes you.'

'Does she? I'm glad. I like her too. She's an unusual woman. It must've been hard for her to give up her friends and family like that to come here.'

'Think so? You'd be just as determined if you made up your mind.' There was curiosity in his voice when he asked, 'Why do you think it was hard for her?'

'Because she told me so.'

He shrugged. 'Perhaps! It was another age, but she thought it was worth it. Things have changed a lot since then. People around here still cling to tradition, but habits have changed a lot. It's not the patriarchal society it used to be. That would bother you? That's a stupid question, isn't it? Of course it would bother you.'

'What do you expect? I'm independent, earning my own money, planning my own life. I don't like the idea of giving all that up to become a man's chattel.'

The silence was marked for a moment. 'A chattel? You're at my beck and call, and that of the other people who hire you.'

'That's completely different; I'm *paid* to be at someone's beck and call, and I choose my employers. I suspect Italian men see things differently, so you naturally don't see things my way.'

A flash of humour crossed his face, and the following smile softened his features. 'I don't know where you get your ideas from, but my generation aren't all looking for brainless doormats. There's no necessity for anyone to dominate in a good marriage. Love and respect have priority these days.'

Her smile matched his; her eyes were challenging. 'True! But would you ever share the driving seat with your wife? Somehow I think sparks would fly all the time.'

His smile vanished; astonishment flitted across his handsome features. With dry amusement, he said, 'I may be difficult at times — who isn't? — but I'm not a human bulldozer. Why shouldn't I make an effort to meet someone I love halfway?'

Her cheeks felt hot, but she ploughed on. 'Because you've never had to, and it gets harder, not easier, the older you get. You're free as a bird, always have been, and you'll find it difficult, if not impossible, to change your attitude.'

He threw back his head and chuckled. He looked young, and she wished he were always so relaxed and happy. Rebecca noticed the chauffeur watching them in the mirror.

'I assure you, I'm prepared to do anything necessary.' He grinned. 'Well, almost anything!'

'I hope so, otherwise heaven help your wife.' She avoided his face to study the buildings flashing past. She guessed they were near the outskirts of the town.

'We're not far from my grandmother's, but I want to stop to see someone. I don't come this way often, so the chance is too good to miss. I won't be long.'

'Of course!' She bent her head and studied the street as the car lessened speed.

He reached for a folder resting in the side pocket and gave their driver a sign. The car drew to a smooth halt. Rebecca decided it wasn't an affluent area. The houses lining the street were tidy but nondescript, with little to recommend them. She was curious why Luca needed to visit someone here.

He crossed the road quickly, his long legs striding determinedly towards a small house with a bright blue door. Rebecca watched him knock. The door opened, and a dainty woman with jet-black hair and an attractive figure appeared. She recognized Luca, and as she stepped out onto the doorstep, a smile spread across her features. She spoke excitedly, her hands fluttering like butterflies in the air. Luca leaned forward and smiled at her. He stuck the folder under his arm and took the young woman's hands between his before he followed her indoors. The door closed and Rebecca felt utterly confused.

8

Suddenly, all pleasure had gone, like whips of clouds that disappear on a sunny day. She tried to swallow the hurt and ignore her disillusionment. She closed her eyes briefly. She reminded herself she was independent and had a good life. She had no right to be jealous! If Luca Barsetti had a girlfriend living in the suburbs, it was none of her business. It wasn't likely that the woman was a close acquaintance of the Barsetti family if she lived here. Luca and the woman knew each other very well, that was obvious.

She locked her hands tightly and was glad that she'd kept her love for him hidden. She felt suffocated and opened the door. She walked along the walls of the houses, knowing the chauffeur was watching her from the car. She wanted to be alone.

The houses sagged against one another; the alleyways were narrow and blanketed in shadows. A noise caught her attention. She was grateful for any diversion, and screwed up her eyes to stare into the shadows. She followed the sound, and found a dog cowering next to a wall. Rebecca went towards it and bent down to let the dog take in her scent. It was in a sorry state. Its tan coat was lustreless, and its body was thin and emaciated. It licked her hand and gazed at her with pleading eyes. It made no attempt to stand up, and then Rebecca noticed that one of its back legs was deformed and matted with dried blood. Her parents had always had dogs, and she couldn't bear to see one injured and abandoned like this. What could she do?

Luca came looking for her. She was too busy worrying about the dog to worry about interrupting him. The chauffeur must have fetched him. Rebecca hadn't asked him to come. His eyes grasped the situation quickly, and he stared at the bundle of misery at her feet.

Eyebrows fractionally raised, he said, 'Oh, no! Don't tell me!'

She rose from the dog that was curled up on the dusty floor. 'I think it's broken its leg. Perhaps a car hit it, or someone was just brutally cruel. I can't leave it!'

'Be sensible! You can't pick up a stray injured dog. Perhaps it belongs to someone locally.'

Rebecca looked around briefly, and bent to stroke the dog's head. 'It isn't a fresh wound; the blood is matted. Someone would have already found if he was from here. Anyway, he's too thin and neglected to belong to anyone.' She straightened and looked at him defiantly. 'I'm not leaving him here. If he doesn't get help, he'll die.'

He tried to block her intention. 'Woman, do you know what you're doing? You're making yourself responsible for a stray dog that no one wants. You live in London, remember?'

She ignored him and showed her determination. 'He needs a vet. That's step number one. Once he's had treatment, I'll think about step number two. I'll do whatever is necessary!'

He tipped his head to the side, and in a desperate attempt to make her change her mind, said warningly, 'Treatment will be expensive, very expensive.'

The light of battle was in her face. 'Don't worry! You don't need to get involved. I don't care what you say, I don't intend to leave him like this. It would be inhumane to walk away. Go on without me. I'll find a taxi, take him to a vet, and come to your gran's later.' She didn't have a clue how far they were from a main road, a taxi, or a vet, but problems were there to be solved. She threw back her head in a small gesture of defiance. 'I'll come as soon as I've settled something. I'm sure she'll understand if you explain.'

He watched her for a second before he lifted his hands in resignation. His inborn characteristics of leadership took over, and although he didn't completely understand how, he found himself catapulted into the middle of an animal rescue attempt. 'Oh, all right! Tell the chauffeur to put a blanket on the back seat.' He looked appraisingly at the dishevelled creature curled in a heap at her feet. 'My father will have a heart attack when he hears we used his favourite limousine as an animal ambulance.' Despite his verbal onslaught, he dropped down to reassure the dog with a few words of Italian. The straggly tail thumped weakly on the floor.

Rebecca guessed Luca was figuring out how to pick up the poor creature without ruining his suit. Shrugging, he accepted the inevitable, and slipped his hands under the slim body. Trying not to touch the injured leg, he lifted the mongrel with as much care as he could. The dog remained silent. Luca was relieved, and silently admitted to himself that he needed no further proof he was going totally mad.

She watched him, thinking that he

although he was a ruthless business-man, he was also kinder than anyone imagined. Holding the weight of the dog with ease in his muscled arms, he eyed her expressively as she stood idly observing him.

'Rebecca! The limousine! The blanket!'

'Oh, yes, I'm sorry. I was lost in thought.' She belly-flopped back to earth and hurried towards the car. The chauffeur stared at her with unblinking eyes when Rebecca told him what to do. She wondered if he'd understood, but he had. His servile mask slipped for a moment as he spread the rug over the seat with an anxious expression on his face. He was too well-trained to question orders. She had an urge to chuckle. She'd put the cat among the pigeons, to save a dog.

Walking towards the waiting car, Luca felt the dog's warm tongue lick his hand. He looked up at the sky and murmured into thin air, 'Don't thank me, you mangy animal, thank that mule-headed woman over there.' The dog picked up the indulgent tone in his voice, and laid his head contentedly across the strong arm. Reaching the car, Luca deposited his burden on the blanketed seat, and tried in vain to restore the sleeves of his jacket to their former pristine condition.

'An old schoolfriend of mine is a vet; we'll take him there.'

Rebecca was relieved that he wasn't arguing any more. She nodded. She didn't understand what Luca told the chauffeur, but he opened the glove compartment and they began to look at a map. Rebecca guessed he was looking for the quickest route.

'I have to say goodbye to someone first.'

Rebecca's attention was drawn once more to the attractive dark-haired woman standing in the doorway, her arms crossed in front of her chest. She heard them talking, and then gave a soft, tinkling laugh. The woman looked curiously in her direction, and Rebecca turned away to settle in the corner next to the dog. He licked her hand and stared at her with sad and woeful eyes.

She understood perfectly how he felt.

Minutes later, Luca joined her again, and got in the passenger seat next to the chauffeur. She held her breath, didn't trust herself to speak, and stroked the dusty dog at her side. She avoided her boss's eyes in the mirror, and didn't look where they were going; it wasn't important.

They stopped in front of an imposing-looking house with a flight of wide marble steps. He lifted the dog out of the car effortlessly again, although it probably wasn't easy. She followed him up the steps and listened passively to his conversation with a white uniformed assistant. His words sent her rushing off to look for her boss. Rebecca waited motionless next to him; she resisted the urge to stroke the dog again. Footsteps echoed along the corridor and a dark-haired, lanky young man, with a thin face and sporting metal-rimmed spectacles, hurried to join them. He smiled easily, and nodded in Luca's direction before breaking into a torrent of rapid Italian.

Luca explained what had happened, and Rebecca's determination to get involved.

The young vet offered Rebecca his hand. It was warm and firm. 'My name is Donato Bellini. I'm very pleased to meet you.' He cast a swift, expert eye over the burden in Luca's arms. 'He looks undernourished and neglected, but his eyes are bright, that's a good sign. His leg is the main problem. I'll take an X-ray straight away, but from the look of it it's almost certainly broken.'

'I thought so when I found him.' She didn't want him to think this was Luca's idea, and she explained, 'I couldn't leave him there.'

Luca added, 'My grandmother is expecting us; can you handle this on your own and let us know the results later on?'

Donato nodded. 'Bring him through to the surgery. This way! Once I've examined him, I'll be able to give you the details. I think I have your private number, Luca, but give it to my receptionist again, just in case.'

They trailed after him; Luca deposited the dog on a central table and the vet made a cursory examination. 'We'll set the leg and check him properly. Once he gets something to eat and drink, he'll soon perk up again, I'm sure.' He stroked the dog's body, and Rebecca was satisfied the animal was in good hands.

Dr. Bellini asked, 'What will happen when he's fit again?'

Rebecca said quickly, 'Is there a chance of finding him a home? I'm only visiting.'

He searched the pocket of his white coat for a stethoscope. 'That won't be easy. My clientele is upper-bracket, and they are not likely to want a pet of unknown origins.'

'But he's a lovely dog!'

He shrugged. 'Some people don't consider 'lovely' a qualification when they look for a dog. They're only interested if the animal fits their image.

I'll ask around, but there are so many stray dogs, it's really difficult . . . '

The 'I told you so' look in Luca's eyes only increased her determination.

'Well, if you can't find anyone, I'll take him back to the UK with me.' Rebecca thought briefly about the ban on animals in her present block of flats. With a brave face, she knew her mother would help if all else failed.

'How?' Luca's voice sounded curious and amused.

'By plane, I suppose.'

His eyebrows rose; the meaning of his expression was clear. 'Have you the slightest idea of all the administrative rigmarole it entails to move a dog from Italy to Britain? There'll be rooms full of forms and paperwork. And the cost will be horrendous.'

'I'm sure Dr. Bellini will find out what I have to do, won't you?' She gave the young man a pleading smile.

The vet looked at her and then at his friend. To his surprise, he found himself nodding.

She looked at Luca in triumph, but Luca Barsetti didn't give up easily. He reminded her brutally, 'Meantime, you have to pay kennel costs. The dog has a broken leg; bones need time to heal!' He paused, studied her face, and resigned himself to his fate. 'Send me the bill, Donny!'

Her eyes were stormy, and although she was secretly awed by the prospect of the possible costs, she swallowed hard and stuck out her chin determinedly. 'You will do no such thing, Dr. Bellini. He's my responsibility; I chose to save him, I'll pay. I'm here for a while, then I go back to London.' She indicated to the assistant to give her the pad and pencil, and she noted her London address. 'Any bills come to me. The only other alternative is to have him put down. No! I'll pay what it takes to give him a decent life. He has a good character. Look at him; even though he's in pain and needs food and water, he's not aggressive! He's grateful for our help, and he deserves a chance.'

Luca turned his eyes to heaven, and gave an audible sigh before he shrugged his shoulders. The young vet gave him a swift slap on the back and smiled at him as they spoke together in Italian. Luca placed his hand under Rebecca's elbow.

'Come on, my grandmother's waiting. Your dog is in good hands.'

Rebecca stroked the dog's head once more, and shook hands with the vet before she followed Luca obediently to the car. They continued the journey in silence; she looked out unseeingly at the passing scenery, until his voice cut in on her thoughts.

'I don't know whether to admire your persistence, or despair of your stubbornness. Why is the dog so important?'

'I love animals. I don't see why he should suffer if I can help. If you don't understand that, there's no point in trying to explain.'

For a couple of minutes, Rebecca's thoughts circled around the dog, and what she'd taken on. She forgot Luca's girlfriend in the suburbs for a while, but the pinpricks of disenchantment soon returned. At last, she registered that the car had come to a halt. They'd driven through busy traffic, and were now on the outskirts of the town, parked outside the entrance to a large house.

She was glad he couldn't read her mind when he offered his hand. She picked up her shoulder bag and slid across the leather seat, pretending to look away. She came to her feet in one quick, effortless movement. She wanted to avoid contact. He looked puzzled, let his hand fall to his side again, and turned away. Rebecca thanked the chauffeur politely as he handed Luca her overnight bag. The man touched the peak of his hat. Rebecca noticed how he gingerly folded the rug and took it with him to the front before he drove off.

Luca's grandmother's house had a boundary wall, painted in bright ochre. The wrought-iron entrance gates opened onto a short crazy-paving path that wandered drunkenly through a small verdant garden to some half-circular steps. Luca supported her elbow with his free hand as they climbed them. Rebecca wished that she had enough gumption to shake it off. The doorbell echoed, and a middle-aged woman opened the door and smiled. Her gaze wandered from Luca to Rebecca with warm and friendly eyes.

'Come in! She's impatient, and waiting for you in the small sitting room.'

'Maria, this is Rebecca Summer — and her luggage. Rebecca, this is Maria, the heart of the house.'

Rebecca smiled automatically. 'Hello, Maria! Pleased to meet you!'

She shook Rebecca's hand briefly. 'My pleasure! I'll take your bag up, and show you your room later. You'd better go straight in.'

Rebecca followed Luca as he strode across the marble floor to open one of the doors leading from the circular hallway; he stood aside to let her pass.

'At last! Where have you been? I expected you a long time ago. Hello, Rebecca!' She pushed herself up from a winged chair, where she'd been sitting, to embrace Rebecca briefly. The genuine warmth of her welcome helped to banish Rebecca's depression. She hugged her and smiled. 'Thank you for inviting me.'

The older woman laughed contentedly. 'I'm glad you're here. Hello, Luca!'

'Hello, Grandma!' He bent and kissed her soundly on her cheek. His smile was spontaneous and sincere. He explained why they were a little late.

Mrs Barsetti smiled benignly at Rebecca. 'That was kind of you. Perhaps the vet will find the dog a good home; if not, it can come here until you think of a solution. It will save you expensive kennelling fees.'

Luca leaned back into an easy chair and listened to the two women with an amused expression on his face.

'Oh, I couldn't impose on you; a dog is a lot of work.'

'Nonsense! Perhaps I can't walk long distances anymore, but lots of short trips would do me good. We used to have a lovely spaniel called Rex. Remember him, Luca?' He nodded resignedly. 'I love dogs, but you get too attached, and at my age it's not sensible to take on a young animal. What happens to them when you die?' Mrs Barsetti busied herself pouring tea. 'Yes, I think I'd enjoy having a dog. Dogs are wonderful company. No arguments! If the vet doesn't find anyone, the dog comes here — until you decide what's to be done with it, of course.'

She asked Luca what he'd been doing before Rebecca could protest. They started to talk about people whose names meant nothing to Rebecca. She was glad to sit back and let her thoughts wander. A few moments later, she jumped when Mrs Barsetti tapped her gently on her knee.

'Rebecca? Rebecca, you're miles away. I just asked you something, but you didn't hear a word I said, did you?'

Rebecca blushed. 'No. Sorry! I was thinking about something else.'

'Well, it must be something important. Just as well that we have plenty of time for a proper chat before you leave on Sunday.'

Rebecca stared at him. 'Sunday? I thought we were returning tomorrow?'

'No. It's better to travel on Sundays. Is there a special reason why you want to go back to San Andrea tomorrow?'

'No, but I don't want to outstay my welcome. It's kind of your Gran to offer me somewhere to stay tonight, but . . .'

'Don't worry, my dear, I seldom have any staying visitors these days, and I have servants who do all the work. It's a pleasure to have you as my guest.' She looked at her jewelled wristwatch. 'Luca, we'll see you tonight.'

He laughed softly. 'Marching orders?'

She nodded, and her grandson stood up, understanding it was time to leave.

Rebecca's bedroom was charming, decorated in tones of apricot with white furniture. She discovered Maria was housekeeper and companion to Luca's grandmother. She'd run the house for many years, and had already unpacked Rebecca's bag when Rebecca went upstairs. Rebecca was stumped; it was a new experience to have someone she didn't even know attend to her needs. She stepped onto the narrow balcony overlooking the garden and breathed in the fragrance of the bushes and plants below. A soft knock on the door heralded the return of Maria. She was holding the dress Rebecca intended to wear that evening.

'I presumed that this is what you'll wear tonight, and thought I'd iron out the creases. I hope I did the right thing?' She smiled at Rebecca.

'How kind of you! You spoil me with so much attention. I just hope it's suitable; it's the only dress I have with me that might be appropriate.'

Maria held the cream, ankle-length, silk-and-linen dress with its painted flowers at arm's length, and appraised it with knowing eyes. 'It's just right; elegant and romantic.' She twisted the hanger and watched the material as the dress fell back into shape again.

Rebecca breathed a sigh of relief. 'I

don't attend formal parties very often.'

'Oh, this evening is a very relaxed gathering of family and friends. When Rose — Mrs Barsetti — was younger, they were elaborate affairs. She enjoys seeing old friends very much, and her charity fetes are wonderful opportunities for that. She doesn't invite lots of business acquaintances now as she did when Mr Barsetti was still alive. Can I get you anything else?'

Rebecca shook her head vigorously. 'I'm sure you've thought of everything. Thank you, Maria.'

Maria brushed her thanks aside with a smile. 'You're welcome.'

After Maria left, Rebecca stretched out on the soft cover of the bed and thought about Luca. She consoled herself with the thought that her job would end soon. Images of Luca with the dark-haired beauty upset her more than she cared to admit. There wasn't just Antonia in his life, there was this other woman . . . and how many more? She forced herself to think about work, about home, about the dog. If the dog came here to Luca's grandmother, for a while it would think it had landed in heaven.

She was glad that she'd never showed Luca how much she cared. Apart from the kiss on the raft, he'd never manipulated her into a situation where she might have been tempted to give in. A couple more weeks, and then she'd never need to see him again.

Her well-meant intentions of banning him from her thoughts hadn't worked. Instead, she knew that she loved him and had never stopped loving him, but he didn't want a serious relationship with any woman. Even if she attracted him, she wouldn't hold his interest for long. Knowing that would help to get her through the remaining days, and she'd leave at the end with her head held high.

9

The darkness was descending, and the house was full of bustle and noise when Rebecca came down the stairs. Her strappy cream sandals tapped on the marble floor, but the sound was lost amid the general hubbub. She hesitated for a moment amongst the crowd of strange faces, and then went towards Luca's grandmother who was standing in the dining room doorway.

She was talking to a distinguished-looking elderly man with grey hair. 'Ah, there you are, Rebecca.'

Giving her a warm smile, Rebecca handed her the illustrated book about England that Jennifer had sent her. 'This is to say thank you for the invitation.'

Mrs Barsetti took it and flipped through some of the pages. 'Beautiful! I'll enjoy looking at this when all the fuss is over.'

Rebecca handed her another envelope with a cheque. 'That's for the orphanage fund.'

'Thank you for both.' Mrs Barsetti placed the book on a nearby table, and the envelope into a glass bowl with lots of others. She held Rebecca at arm's length for a moment.

'You look lovely, my dear. Oh . . . this is an old friend of mine, General Arber. Ken has lived in Italy for years and years. He was a good friend of my husband. They shared the same hobby; they were both passionate deep-sea anglers.'

'How do you do, General?' Rebecca held out her hand and felt it enclosed in a firm grip. 'What's so special about Italy? What keeps you here?'

He laughed. 'Oh, lots and lots of things. Apart from the weather, which is my main reason, there are all sorts of other attractions. I've lived here for nearly fifteen years, and I don't regret a day. You work for Luca?'

'Yes, but only temporarily.'

'How do you like it?'

Rose Barsetti laughed and fingered the gold-and-emerald necklace around her neck. The emeralds flashed like spears of vivid green. 'Rebecca won't tell you what she really thinks. I've already asked her.'

He shook his head. 'I'm talking about Italy, not Luca.'

'Oh, I like it very much. I've only seen San Andrea this time, but I went on a coach trip to Rome once. Everywhere is full of history. It's absolutely amazing.'

'Ah, San Andrea! It's a good place, isn't it? I spent many happy days there with Leandro. We often used it as a base when we went fishing together. What a place to work! Hope Luca gives you some time off to explore the island?'

Rebecca didn't want to even listen to Luca's name. 'What a beautiful necklace, Mrs Barsetti.'

She fingered it lovingly. 'Yes, it is, isn't it? It's one of my favourites. Leandro gave it to me on our seventh wedding anniversary. It was the first really expensive piece of jewellery he bought me, so it's very special. I don't have much opportunity to wear it these days.'

Some other guests arrived, so Rebecca and the general moved aside. He was clearly fond of Mrs Barsetti, and spoke in admiring terms about her husband. A waiter offered them a tray of drinks. Rebecca took a dry sherry and the general helped himself to whiskey.

'Rose says you're based in London. I must say that women nowadays lead very different lives to those of my generation.'

'We get more chances to do what we like — but there were always independent women; even fifty, a hundred, or a thousand years ago.'

'Perhaps, but it was never quite as easy to be independent, as it is now. Wanting a career, plus a home and family, was an exception in my day. It was considered going against the grain . . . admittedly, mainly by men!' He smiled, and brushed his moustache into shape with an upward movement of one finger. 'Lord, I wish I was thirty again! Your generation have the world at their feet; they only need to have a sense of adventure.'

He knew London very well, and paid frequent visits to see family and friends. He talked and listened with interest to Rebecca's description of her family and her job. He was Rebecca's notion of an old-fashioned military gentleman. The dining room was a magnificent place filled with highly polished antique furniture. Candles shimmered along the length of the long dining table. It was formally laid for the evening meal with silver cutlery, crystal glasses and exquisite porcelain.

Among the bustle of people already gathered, Rebecca didn't spot Luca straight off, but told herself she didn't want to see him anyway. Eventually, a gap in the throng showed him talking to someone at the far end of the long room. He looked extremely handsome in a black tuxedo, and her heartbeat increased. He sensed her eyes on him, and lifted his glass in a gesture of familiarity. She didn't react, and the gap closed again before she had time to be glad, or to regret, that she hadn't responded. To her own dismay, despite everything, she still wished she was by his side.

People began to assemble for dinner. Rebecca and the general discovered they were on opposite ends of the table, so they parted company. Rebecca sat down on one of the evenly spaced dining chairs, and was pleased to find Marco on one side of her, and a member of the British business community, a tall man with a fresh complexion and disciplined hair, on the other.

He introduced himself. 'Good evening! I'm Clive Oliver.' He leaned forward to read her place card. 'Rebecca Summer. Related to Mrs Barsetti? I haven't seen you here before.'

Marco came to her aid. 'Rebecca is a friend of the family, Clive.'

Rebecca thought that the term

'friend of the family' was an exaggeration, but she didn't correct him.

Clive nodded, and pulled nervously at his bow tie. 'I almost didn't make it on time. The traffic is terrible at this time of day. It's a miracle that it doesn't collapse . . . '

Rebecca smiled politely and shook out her serviette.

'It's my own fault, I know it's sheer madness to take a taxi, but if I don't, I can't drink.' He added for Rebecca's benefit, 'The drivers are crazy, and some of them even pick up additional passengers on the way, although it's not allowed. There's no point in getting annoyed, it doesn't make any difference.'

Rebecca saw Luca, half way down the table, with Chiara on one side and an unknown woman on the other. At present, he was talking to the stranger. She spotted Luca's parents and Antonia too. Luca's mother met her eye and lifted her hand to wave briefly. Rebecca smiled back and reciprocated. Antonia saw her, but sent Rebecca a cool glance that expected, and got, no reaction. She'd never forgive Rebecca for the episode on San Andreas. She looked extraordinarily beautiful, like she'd just stepped off the front page of *Vogue*.

The meal was provided, and served, by outside caterers. There were small portions of smoked salmon and melon, sole in a cream sauce with asparagus, an Italian dish of vegetables and lamb, a sweet lemon dessert, the whole lot rounded off with cheeses, fresh fruit and coffee. Spread over a couple of hours, it was a pleasant meal. Rebecca could talk freely to Marco, and found that Clive Oliver wasn't as insipid as she'd first believed. He'd been to several interesting places, and he was an entertaining storyteller.

Marco wanted to know how her agency functioned, and he explained a bit about the complicated structure of the Barsetti businesses and its many subsidiaries and partnerships. She found that time flew. When the meal ended, they parted company. Marco was whisked off by an acquaintance, and Clive went to talk to someone he knew nearby. People wandered into the sitting room, into the hall where drinks were being served, or out onto the terrace. She thought she saw Luca coming in her direction, but Antonia caught his arm and pulled him aside. Rebecca heard her throaty laugh floating across the room.

Suddenly Chiara caught her arm. 'Rebecca! I saw Gran put you next to Marco. I hope he took care of you?'

'Your husband is a paragon, you know that very well!'

Chiara smiled smugly. 'He's not bad, is he? How are you? When I told the children you'd be here tonight, they sent their best wishes. Gabriella told me to say hello, twice!'

'That's nice. Give them my love. Gabriella's a little gem.'

'Ah, well!' Chiara laughed. 'You seem to like children. Italians spoil their children; the smaller they are, the more people spoil them. Gabriella knows that, and is already very adept at using her charms.' She hooked her arm through Rebecca's as they wandered aimlessly around the rooms. 'How long are you staying?'

'Until Sunday, I think.'

'If you're not doing anything, come and visit me tomorrow morning. We can have a cup of coffee, or we'll go shopping.'

Rebecca was non-committal. She didn't fancy trailing round shops, but didn't say so. 'That's kind, but I don't know if your grandmother has planned anything. I'll have to ask her first. She's very busy this evening, I'll let you know.'

'Fine; you have my telephone number? Ring tomorrow morning after breakfast.'

An acquaintance caught Chiara's attention and she moved off. Luca would soon spot her, even in this crowd; he was taller than most of the men present. He probably thought it was his duty to entertain her. She'd find a secluded spot, until she could politely withdraw.

She crossed paths with his mother on

the way. Normally Rebecca wouldn't have interrupted, but if Luca was looking, he'd leave her with his mother. She wouldn't be able to avoid him when they got back to San Andrea, but she needed to adjust to the knowledge that he really was the womanizer the papers alleged he was.

'Mrs Barsetti. Good evening! How are you?'

'Rebecca! Nice to see you! Are you enjoying yourself?'

'Yes. It was extremely kind of your mother-in-law to invite me.'

'Rose loves company, she always has. I know that she particularly wanted you to come this evening. Oh — this is Arianne Platini, a good friend of mine.'

'Pleased to meet you, Mrs Platini. I don't want to interrupt, I only wanted to say hello!'

'You're not interrupting. Are you looking for Luca? I just saw him going into the hallway.'

Rebecca nodded and smiled her thanks, and made a polite escape in the opposite direction. She headed towards the sitting room. Rebecca skirted round people until she reached the open French windows. She watched some couples dancing in the centre of the room. Cooler air enticed her to move outside into the garden.

On the way, she bumped into Clive again. 'All, Miss Summer! Would you like to dance?'

Luca materialized out of nowhere and caught her hand; she had no time to think clearly or react. 'Sorry, Clive, but she's promised this dance to me; haven't you, Rebecca?'

She was open-mouthed and speechless; but he manoeuvred her onto the dance floor before she'd closed her lips. He was a good dancer, his steps were easy to follow, and despite all her intentions, Rebecca admitted it was heaven to feel his arm encircling her body and holding her tight.

'Are you avoiding me, by any chance?' He guided her purposefully out onto the flagged terrace. He manoeuvred her to where the shadows were strongest. Branches of a tree dipped to hide them from the people inside. In the darkness, he towered over her. Rebecca waited for him to release her. Her insides were still churning, and his nearness made her heart beat too fast. He pulled her even closer. She had the feeling she couldn't breathe properly. Time stood still and all her determined efforts to avoid looking up into his face ended in failure. Her communication skills seemed to have deserted her completely too, and her flesh prickled where his hands touched her bare skin. She'd never experienced such sexual attraction before; no one had ever roused her in this way (she'd imagined it in her dreams years ago, but reality was better). Something triggered hidden wants and needs in a way she didn't believe possible. Warm desire blossomed, and she wondered why Luca had this kind of power over her. Utter confusion reigned, and she tried to pull herself together. The effects of the heat and the closeness of their bodies did nothing to help calm her. Rebecca swallowed and forced herself to speak. 'That wasn't fair. Mr Oliver was trying to be kind to someone on their own.'

'Kind, my hat! He fancies you!'

Laughter bubbled somewhere inside, and for a silly second or two she felt ridiculously happy. His eyes were twinkling bright spots in the half-darkness. Her voice broke slightly as she tried to answer. 'Really? I'm flattered.'

There was a pause before he put his hand under her chin and lifted her face. It was a surprise, and yet expected; the feel of his lips on hers sent a hot wave through her body. She was shocked by her own emotions and she felt his heart thudding against her own. His face was half-hidden in shadow, but his proximity, their physical contact, made her senses swim. She knew she should pull away, but a stronger emotion glued her to the spot. She couldn't think straight, and felt the heady sensation of his lips against her neck and the hollow at the base of her throat. His lips recaptured hers, and this time they were more demanding. She had an overwhelming desire for him, and wanted the moment to never end.

Somewhere, from the garden, or from the house, the sound of voices broke the spell, and she surfaced from a frenzy of just wanting him. Struggling with herself, her conscience pricked her even though she wanted to give anything he asked for. There was satisfaction in knowing he found her attractive, but common sense triumphed in the end. What was she doing? She found strength to push his chest with her hands, and stared at him with chaos in her eyes. Why would someone like Luca want someone like her, unless it was just for a short-lived, cheap affair? The black-haired beauty from this afternoon might accept that, but she wouldn't. She needed complete commitment. If she gave in now, it would lead nowhere. He'd leave her after an emotional adventure between the sheets.

They stood rooted to the spot, both of them paralysed. He reached out, but Rebecca avoided his hands and moved back.

'This is foolish.' Her breath was uneven, and her face was aflame.

'Is it? Why?' His question was sharp and pointed, and he sounded nervous.

Rebecca could almost believe he was almost as confused as she was. It took an effort to control her rebellious emotions. 'You're my employer. This isn't right or fitting.'

They faced each other silently. The atmosphere was strained and unresolved. He could see Rebecca's face better than she could his; he stood with his back to the sparse light. ''Right and fitting'? That sounds like something from the nineteenth century.' He gave a short, sharp laugh. 'This is the twenty-first; these things happen.' He shrugged and his voice sounded harsh. 'What's so wrong? It may not be the most perfect or most appropriate moment, but . . . '

She swallowed the despair in her throat. She couldn't face finding out how far he could manipulate her. 'I . . . excuse me!' She turned and fled, walking away swiftly without waiting to hear any more.

She almost pushed her way through the throng, her face a stiff mask; glad that she didn't meet anyone she knew on the way. She was shaking, and leaned against the door in relief when she reached her bedroom. Sitting on the edge of the bed, she crumpled the material of her dress in her clenched fists, closed her eyes, and hoped things would be back to normal again tomorrow.

10

'Mrs Barsetti is still sleeping.'

Rebecca looked up from the table. 'I'm not surprised.'

Maria nodded. 'Do you need anything else?'

Rebecca waved at the loaded table in front of her. 'Who could ask for more?'

'The catering company is here to collect everything and put the rooms in order again, so I thought it was best to put you on the terrace.'

'You make it sound like as if it was some kind of punishment.' Rebecca smiled at her. 'Breakfast like this is sheer luxury for me.'

The housekeeper smiled. 'Good. If you need anything — ?'

Rebecca reassured her. 'I'll come and look for you.'

Maria hurried into the house to oversee the team of people restoring it to its former appearance. Rebecca leaned back, and wished she could do more justice to Maria's efforts, but she wasn't hungry. She was still churned up inside, and couldn't face food. She managed a slice of dry toast and coffee. Hooking the handle of the cup with her finger as she lifted it to her lips, the coffee was hot and strong, and it tasted good. She hadn't slept well. Her mirror this morning had showed a pale, tired face.

'Rebecca! Luca is on the phone. He wants to pick you up later. Is that alright?'

Rebecca's stomach did a somersault. Her brain reacted quicker than her heart. 'Oh, what a pity! I . . . I've already arranged to go out later this morning.'

'He wants to invite you for lunch, and to show you his house.' The expression on Maria's face gave nothing away.

Rebecca's brain somersaulted. Just the two of them, in his house? Alone? No — that wasn't a good idea! She couldn't cope at the moment. 'Will you please say I'm sorry, but I have a previous appointment?'

Chiara was happy when Rebecca phoned to say she'd like to come. She collected her in her Mercedes, and Rebecca trailed after her through several boutiques. Chiara wasn't looking for anything in particular, but found a beautiful hand-painted silk scarf and a string of coral beads that were 'a perfect match for a silk dress I bought last week in Brindisi'. After a brief stop to buy some cosmetics, Rebecca was relieved when Chiara suggested they return home for some coffee. Chiara and Marco's bungalow was beautiful. It had a kidney-shaped turquoise swimming pool, and a lovely small garden.

Rebecca was glad to sink back into the soft leather sofa in the large air-conditioned sitting room. 'Where are the children? I was hoping to see them again.'

'Birthday party! They're having a good time at the moment, I expect.

Perhaps you'll see them before you leave. Like something to eat?'

Rebecca shook her head vigorously. 'Thanks, although I'd love a cup of coffee.'

Chiara passed on the request to her housekeeper.

'Do you work, Chiara?'

The other woman looked surprised. 'Work? No, I have my hands full with the two children, entertaining people for Luca, and organizing functions when he needs my support.'

'Isn't that boring?'

'No. I enjoy my life. All work is boring once you're used to it. You work as a secretary; I work as a wife. I don't want a career. One person in this house who's addicted to work is more than enough. I try to balance Marco's life by cultivating his family and friends, providing him with somewhere to replenish his energies, and being someone who loves him for himself, not what he represents.'

'When you put it like that, it sounds

as if you've given up your life just to make his comfortable.'

Chiara shrugged. 'Does it? I have no problem with that, if it's true. I love Marco and he loves me. I also enjoy my lifestyle. I live in luxury. I have two happy children and a satisfied husband. Why do I need a job? I'd only take work away from someone who really needs it.'

'It's difficult for me to imagine that anyone in this day and age is prepared to completely bury their own wishes just to please a husband.'

Chiara laughed. 'You'd be surprised how many women are happy to do so, especially when their husbands are top people. Marco and I don't always see eye to eye on everything, but we still have a good marriage. I admire women who have a husband and family, and also work full- or part-time — but I don't need to be one of them, so don't try and give me a bad conscience, because it won't work!'

A thoughtful expression on her face,

Rebecca said, 'Sorry, that wasn't my intention. It's right for you, but I don't think it would be right for me. I've had to work too hard to gain my independence.' Rebecca tilted her head to the side and tried to sound encouraging. 'Tell you what, if my agency ever opens a branch here, I'll give you first chance to be office manager!'

They looked at each other, smiled, and giggled. Chiara was one of life's butterflies, but Rebecca couldn't help liking her. She was intrinsically a very honest and nice person. The sound of a man's heavy tread in the hall interrupted the conversation. Rebecca looked up, expecting to see Marco.

Luca's voice reached them before he entered the room. He stopped in his tracks when he saw them sitting together drinking coffee. Chiara's cosmetics were piled on an occasional table nearby, and his eyes swept over them fractiously. His features hardened. His cold eyes sniped at her. 'Oh, Rebecca? What a surprise! This was your important appointment?'

Rebecca couldn't stop the feeling of delight when she saw him. No matter what she did to smother her feelings, it didn't work when she was close to him. She coloured slightly. 'Yes, Chiara and I arranged to meet last night.' It wasn't completely accurate — they hadn't actually arranged anything till this morning — but thankfully Chiara remained silent. Luca stared at her until she began to feel uncomfortable, then he turned to Chiara.

'I wanted to see Marco.'

'He's at the club with those Americans. He invited them out to lunch; they're flying back to the States on Monday.'

Rebecca had a moment to study his tall, commanding figure. His voice was polite, but Rebecca noted the angry undertone. He thrust his fingers impatiently through his thick hair; it sprang back into place. He proceeded to pointedly ignored Rebecca's presence, and snapped his fingers. 'Oh . . . yes! I'd forgotten. I'll get in touch with him later, or first thing tomorrow morning.'

Chiara looked at her watch. 'Join us for coffee. He could be back soon.'

'No, I won't interrupt your heart-to-heart, and I'll find my own way out.' His dark eyes flashed unspoken messages in Rebecca's direction before he turned swiftly and strode towards the door with determined steps. In the hall, they heard him muttering before the outer door closed with a bang.

Chiara looked amused. 'What's got into him, I wonder?'

Rebecca tried to look indifferent. 'No idea.'

'Sure? I've seldom seen him that worked up before. Luca usually has it all under control.'

'Really?' Rebecca stared at the dregs in her coffee cup.

Chiara speculated silently, and finally asked, 'Rebecca, what's this about? You know, don't you?'

Rebecca shrugged vaguely. 'No. Why should I?'

Chiara drew imaginary circles on the

shiny surface of the glass table. 'Tell me to mind my own business, but is something going on between you two? Whenever you're together there's a kind of electricity in the air.'

Rebecca attempted, a weak laugh. 'Chiara! You have a vivid imagination. He's my boss.'

'What was that remark about an 'important appointment'? He sounded put out.'

'He's probably just in a bad mood.'

Chiara didn't give up so easily. 'What did he mean about 'appointment'?'

Rebecca conceded defeat and explained. 'I expect he meant that he invited me to visit his house this morning, but I told him I was meeting you. He probably didn't like it. He automatically always expects people to fall in with his plans, doesn't he?'

Chiara was lifting a cup to her lips and she spluttered. 'Luca invited you? To his house? And you refused?' She replaced it in the saucer with a loud clatter. 'Do you know what you've done?'

Rebecca looked puzzled. 'No. What?'

'Hardly anyone has had an invitation to visit him there. I know that Antonia has never been inside, despite all her efforts.' Chiara suddenly realised with blinding clarity that Marco's initial hunch about Luca and Rebecca was right. 'And you turned him down?'

Rebecca looked towards the window. 'I'm only his temporary secretary. There is no reason for him to include me in the private side of his life. It's better that I don't see too much of him.' Rebecca was pleased to find a logical excuse. 'If the press finds out I've worked for him, they might hound me for information about him. Mrs Barsetti senior has been very kind, you've been kind — the Barsetti family are all generous people. I could unwittingly supply them with information about your private lives. What I don't know, I can't tell!'

'Luca is very proud of that house. He even helped to drill away some of the rock one summer so that the house could be positioned just where it is, overlooking the surrounding countryside . . . '

Rebecca didn't want to think about Luca working with a pneumatic drill — it produced images of a muscled body straining to do a good job.

' . . . although he doesn't spend much time there; he more or less lives in London these days.'

'He lives in London, permanently?' Rebecca's voice faded to a half-whisper.

'Yes, didn't you know?' Chiara was amused. They didn't seem to know very much about each other. 'He has an absolutely fabulous two-level bachelor apartment in the Docklands. He bought up a whole building, before the redevelopment plans took off. He sold it for an unbelievable amount and he still owns a huge penthouse apartment at the top of the building. His house here is his Italian refuge, but he lives in London most of the time; because it's the centre of European finances.'

'I didn't realise that.' She fingered

her watchstrap. 'I try not to ask employers too many personal questions.'

Chiara said, 'I would!'

Rebecca couldn't stop herself. 'That's why many of the women who've been linked to him in the gossip columns were British.'

Chiara eyed her carefully. There was no point in trying to mislead Rebecca. 'I don't know how many affairs were serious.' She noticed the flicker in Rebecca's face. 'Marco knows Luca better than anyone else, and he's never said Luca has met someone special. He's never brought a special girl home to introduce her to the family as far as I know.'

Rebecca looked down, listened, and then remarked, 'All the articles about his girlfriends can't be complete lies!' She hurried to add, 'Not that it's my business; he's entitled to have as many girlfriends as he likes.'

Chiara huffed softly in frustration. 'He's not a monk, Rebecca, and I'm sure the press often distort things out of all proportion sometimes. My Marco isn't so vulnerable these days, but Luca is. His private life sells newspapers and magazines.'

She couldn't help herself. 'But he did have an affair with Antonia, didn't he?'

'Oh, Antonia . . . Her parents and his would have welcomed it. I'm sure they now all realize that it was wrong. Especially Marco's parents, after the way she behaved on San Andrea recently. They saw how she was hounding Luca. My mother-in-law told me so. Antonia is too egoistical for Luca. He needs someone who under-stands and supports him. Antonia only cares about one thing — Antonia. Luca deserves better. More coffee?'

Rebecca studied the face of her watch. 'No, thanks! I promised I'd be back for afternoon tea. Would you call me a taxi?'

Chiara nodded and fumbled in a nearby drawer for a small leather book. She called a taxi and sat down again. 'Only take a couple of minutes! I hope

I'll see you again?'

Chiara hoped she'd handled the conversation sensitively. Without knowing whether Luca was really interested or not, she didn't dare encourage Rebecca too much.

Rebecca smiled. 'I hope so too. We could meet next time you're in London. We probably won't meet again here; this job finishes soon.' Rebecca fumbled in her bag and gave Chiara a visiting card. 'My office and private number.'

Chiara accepted the card. 'I'd like that.'

'And I'd enjoy being able to repay your kindness.'

Chiara brushed her thanks aside.

'Remember me to the children. Gabriella and I were talking about Cinderella last time I saw her; tell Gabriella I hope she finds her Prince Charming.' Rebecca thought of her own prince, and of a fairy tale that wouldn't come true.

Chiara smiled. 'I'm already sorry for anyone she sets her cap at.' In the hallway the doorbell sounded. 'Ah!'

A maid opened the door and there were sounds of muted female voices. Antonia entered, wearing a dress cut on perfect lines. Her mass of jet-black hair was pinned back behind her ears and hung loosely to her shoulders. She looked like a Chinese ivory figure. She looked surprised to find Rebecca when she came in. A cloud of expensive perfume wafted around her as she moved.

'Hello, Chiara!' She kissed Chiara on the cheek. She hesitated when she saw Rebecca, but she couldn't be blatantly rude in Chiara's presence. 'Rebecca! What a surprise to find you here! I thought that you'd be on your way back to the island by now.'

'No. Luca wants to return tomorrow. I have no choice in the matter.'

Antonia nodded. Only someone who looked carefully would have noticed her lips thinning. 'I suppose Luca has his reasons, although it seems unnecessary to keep you hanging around.' She tossed her head and turned her attention to Chiara.

'I came to find out if you'd like to come to an art exhibition this evening. An exciting new artist; someone who paints on the bark of trees, mostly women wrapped in veils.'

Chiara made a face.

Antonia hurried to say, 'I know — it sounds slightly mad, doesn't it? That's what I thought too, but everyone is going! Elena gave me a handful of invitations, because she can't make it, so now I'm looking for company. I've promised to go.'

Chiara looked sceptical. 'Marco wanted a night in. I don't know if I can persuade him to sacrifice that, to hob-nob with people he sees all the time.'

Antonia's voice was plaintive. 'Oh, do come! I'm sure you can persuade him. He can laze around tomorrow.'

Chiara looked at Rebecca. 'How many tickets have you got?'

'Six. Why?'

'Who else is invited?'

'Well, if I can persuade you and Marco, I might be able to talk Luca round to going. I tried him this morning, but he wouldn't budge!'

Chiara turned her back on Antonia for a moment. She looked at Rebecca and winked.

'What about Rebecca? She's not doing anything this evening. You can invite her too. I'm sure she'd find it very interesting.'

Rebecca lifted her hand in protest, and the expression on Antonia's face wasn't very encouraging either, but Chiara was on the move.

'If you can persuade Rebecca, I'll try to persuade Marco. If Marco comes, I'll ask him to get Luca to come again.'

Antonia hesitated for a moment. 'Would you like to come, Rebecca?'

It was an invitation of sorts, but without any warmth. Rebecca and Antonia were both still rooted in their mutual dislike. Rebecca pulled her thoughts together. 'Oh, I don't think so, it's not my scene.'

Chiara hassled her. 'Oh, come on, Rebecca! It's sometimes quite interesting. There's always an odd mixture of people, and I'm sure that you'd enjoy it. If you don't come, I won't go, then Marco and Luca won't go either!'

Rebecca felt trapped. She didn't belong here; she'd be gone in a couple of weeks, it didn't really matter if she went or not. 'I don't have anything suitable to wear!'

Chiara sensed success on the horizon. She eyed Rebecca. 'I have just the thing. One of those famous 'little black dresses'. It doesn't fit me anymore, but I'm almost sure it'd fit you!'

Rebecca wished she could think quickly of a watertight excuse, but couldn't. She shrugged.

Chiara was delighted. 'Good! That's settled! What time?'

Antonia was still trying to catch up with Chiara. 'Um! Oh, you know, the usual — any time between eight and nine.' She looked at the clock on the mantelpiece. 'I'll be off. I'll phone Luca and tell him both of you and Rebecca are coming. I'll confirm with you later. I must be off!'

Chiara followed her to the door. When she came back, Rebecca still tried to get out of it. 'Chiara, it's kind of you to include me, but I won't know anyone else. I'll enjoy staying at home with Luca's grandmother just as much.'

'I'm sure! But I think you'll enjoy this more. Who knows — perhaps you'll meet a millionaire, and end up as my next-door neighbour!'

Rebecca couldn't help laughing; Chiara was a really nice person. 'I don't think there's much likelihood of that happening. Millionaires are usually thin on the ground, and they're not looking for women who earn their living as a secretary.'

'Please, Rebecca! I want to go, but not without Marco. I can only talk him round if I can convince him he'll spoil my evening, your evening, Luca's evening *and* Chiara's evening if he doesn't agree.'

Rebecca looked unperturbed. 'Perhaps you could just go with Luca and Antonia?'

'I want to go with Marco.'

Rebecca waited a few seconds. 'Oh, very well! You're a determined person, aren't you?'

Chiara grinned. 'Yes, I am. Come upstairs and try the dress. If it doesn't fit, you can wear the one you wore last night — it's just as suitable.'

Rebecca heard a car hooting. 'That sounds like the taxi.'

Chiara glanced out of the narrow hall window. 'Oh, yes, it's already here. You can take the dress with you and try it on at home. I'll phone and let you when we'll pick you up.'

The dress was found and given. She walked Rebecca to the door and gave the driver directions.

Rebecca looked through the rear window and waved, until the taxi rounded the curve and Chiara was lost to sight.

By the time the taxi dropped her at Luca's grandmother's house, she was sorry she'd given in. Apart from the fact that she wasn't interested in the art exhibition, she'd successfully avoided Luca this morning, and didn't want to be in a group he was with this evening.

She had tea with his gran, and after Mrs Barsetti had rested for a while, they played dominoes. The domino stones clicked as they laid them on the cherrywood table. The only other sound was the regular ticking of the grandfather clock in one of the shady corners.

'So, you enjoyed your visit to Chiara's?' She waited. 'Is something the matter, Rebecca? You're not concentrating. You'll never win if you don't watch your stones.' She smiled at the young woman, turning one of the ivory dominoes in her hand.

Rebecca told her about Antonia's invitation and Chiara's efforts to get her to go. 'I know nothing about this artist, and don't particularly want to either.'

Mrs Barsetti laughed. 'I know what you mean. I doubt whether some of these artists understand what they do themselves some of the time. It's often just an excuse for a group of affluent people to get together and throw their money around for things they don't really want.'

'That's what I mean. I don't belong. I work for a living.'

'Even very rich people work, Rebecca — if they didn't, and failed to keep their eye on the people who are making their money for them, they'd soon be less affluent. You should be proud that you're independent. If — and I say *if* — someone tried to make you think that you 'don't belong', just tell yourself that they're a very stupid person — because they are. That's what I told myself when I got used to a new world when my husband became rich.' She patted Rebecca's hand. 'Go this evening, my dear; enjoy yourself! Think of it as just another experience. If you hate it, call a taxi, and come back here again.'

Rebecca nodded mutely. She'd make the best of it. 'Chiara loaned me a dress.'

Mrs Barsetti nodded. 'Chiara has her heart in the right place. She spends too much money on clothes and jewellery, but some women are shopping-mad. Do you like shopping?'

'Yes, what woman doesn't? But I usually end up buying the same brand all the time.'

Mrs Barsetti nodded. 'I know what you mean. You save yourself a lot of time if you've found a style that suits. You have good taste, Rebecca.' She studied her dominoes with unnecessary care. 'Maria mentioned that Luca invited you to his house this morning, and you turned him down because Chiara had asked you to visit her?'

Rebecca twisted one of the domino stones nervously in her fingers. Was nothing private in this family? 'Yes, I'd already promised Chiara. I don't think Luca was very happy; in fact, when I saw him at Chiara's, I think he was angry with me.'

Mrs Barsetti laughed softly. 'I bet he was. He's used to women who dance at his bidding. Perhaps he thinks you were just trying to gain more attention.'

Rebecca met the older woman's bright blue eyes without wavering. 'Do you believe that? I'm not double-dealing on him for his attention!'

The other woman nodded. 'I believe you. Even if you were chasing him, I wouldn't do anything to stop you, it's none of my business. I just hope you don't get hurt.'

Rebecca coloured and was surprised. They were talking about her grandson.

Mrs Barsetti noticed her reaction. 'I'm a realist. And I say what I think. That is one thing that gets easier with age. Luca isn't perfect husband material, but what really interesting man is? He's difficult, stubborn, determined, and unpredictable ... but he'll do anything for the people he loves, and he'll also be a good husband and father when he finds the right woman. I want him to be happy; he's a wonderful grandson. Essentially he's a good man, like his grandfather was.'

Rebecca looked down and avoided her eyes. 'I'm sure you're right. He'll find the right partner one day, I'm sure.'

'I never interfere, but anyone who knows him well will tell you never to underestimate Luca once he's made up his mind.' She placed another stone on the shiny surface of the table, and looked at her wristwatch. 'Would you ask Maria to make us another cup of tea? I'd love a cup, wouldn't you?'

'Yes.' Rebecca was glad of the excuse to order her thoughts again. 'I'll see if I can find her.'

'She's usually watching television in the library.'

'No cheating — wait until I get back!'

Mrs Barsetti laughed loudly. 'Rebecca! As if I would.'

That evening, Rebecca changed into the black dress. It looked good on her slim frame; it made her skin look like alabaster, her eyes darker. The style was classical and the soft skirt reached just to her knee. It looked as if it had been made for her. She applied more make-up than usual and joined Mrs Barsetti for the evening meal. Chiara and Luca were picking her up. Rebecca toyed with her food because she was still nervous. Mrs Barsetti didn't comment. Afterwards, Rebecca went into the living room with Mrs Barsetti.

'I've got something for you. That dress looks really good on you, and you look wonderful, but you do need something to give it an extra touch.' She took a small blue velvet box from a side-table and opened the lid. Inside was a gold arrow with some small diamonds worked into the feathers on the tail of the shaft. She took it out, placed the case on the table and proceeded to fix the brooch near Rebecca's left shoulder. 'I bought this many, many years ago in Bond Street. I've always liked it, perhaps because I chose it myself, and I remembered it just now. It's just the thing to liven that dress up and give it a special touch.'

'Mrs Barsetti, I can't! The dress is Chiara's; the jewellery is yours. I'm a complete fraud.'

'Don't be silly! Of course you're not. I just want to boost your confidence in yourself, that's all.'

'Chiara will recognise it, or someone else will, and they'll brand me as a cadger!'

Mrs Barsetti laughed. 'I haven't worn it for years. I'm sure they've all forgotten it. Even if someone remembers, it isn't important. I'd like you to wear it. Wear it for me! One English woman supporting another in a foreign country! Go and look in the mirror, it looks just right with the dress, and it suits your personality. It's uncomplicated and classy!'

Rebecca shook her head and smiled before she turned away to study her reflection the large gold-framed mirror in the marbled hallway.

*　*　*

The temperature was very mild; a jacket was superfluous. Chiara, Marco and Rebecca went straight in. The long room was already quite full. White walls displayed a collection of paintings in garish colours, and some sculptures were standing on slender pedestals here and there. Rebecca stayed with Marco and Chiara for a while, but they knew so many people and so many people knew them that Rebecca wandered away to study the paintings. Someone handed them a catalogue as they came in, and Rebecca started to tour the pictures. More and more people arrived and filled the room. Most of them seemed to be more interested in seeing each other than looking at the things on exhibition. There was an atmosphere of opulence and wealth. Jewellery jangled, glasses tinkled, and self-satisfied people preened themselves in the knowledge of belonging.

Rebecca was one of the few who seemed to be actually looking at the paintings. Surprisingly, she liked some of them, because of their colouring. She tried hard to evaluate them using the explanations in the catalogue. It was all too confusing. She gave up, and decided the prices were too exorbitant for what was on offer.

Half way along one of the walls, Rebecca noticed a stir further down the room, and she looked up to see Antonia arriving with Luca. Rebecca was unable to face him and unwilling to turn away. Basking in being the centre of attention, Antonia smiled widely at everyone and kissed everyone on their cheeks. This was the world she loved and needed. She and Luca made their way to where Chiara and Marco were standing, and then Rebecca dragged her eyes away, and forced herself not to look at them any longer. She reminded herself that Luca was being typically generous with himself; yesterday he was with that woman in the suburbs, and today Antonia was his choice. Whose turn would it be tomorrow?

Watching her, anyone would believe Rebecca was a real art expert, but she felt rather out of place. She hated being in the same room as the man she loved, who liked other women more than he did her because she wouldn't give in to his flirting.

Someone carrying a tray of long-stemmed glasses offered her one, and she took it and gulped it down. She moved onto the next painting. It looked like she felt, a mixture of confused emotions and torment.

'Well, hello! I didn't expect to see you here.'

Rebecca looked up at Clive Oliver. She smiled at him, genuinely glad to see someone she knew. 'Hello! How nice to see you again. Yes . . . ' She lowered her voice. 'It's rather like a gathering of the top ten-thousand, isn't it?'

He laughed softly. 'Yes, you're not far from the truth. I think that anyone who is anyone in this town is here tonight.'

The hubbub of noise was growing. Through the gaps of people in motion, she saw Luca watching them for a moment, and she rippled her fingers. His expression was grim and remained so. Rebecca turned her attention hastily back to Clive, and made an immaterial remark about the painting in front of them.

Rebecca stayed with Clive. Either he was glad to have found someone to talk to, or he was flattered by her attention, because he made no effort to go elsewhere. Rebecca was even sorry that she'd thought him insipid yesterday; this evening, he was her port in a sea of storms.

Noticing he was as disinterested in the paintings as she was, she asked, 'Why did you come this evening? I understand the invitations were limited, and it was intended to be an exclusive gathering.' She hastened to add, 'I don't mean that you're not a VIP.'

He laughed. 'No, don't bother to explain. I know what you mean. Our company often gets free invitations, and sometimes I am their representative!'

'Very impressive!'

'Isn't it? I know nothing about art, I'm not even interested, and I don't know many of the people here either. It's not my idea of spending a pleasant evening.'

Rebecca took a sip from her glass. 'Isn't it difficult, always having to mix with strangers and still feel comfortable?'

He shrugged. 'It's part of the job. Sometimes you're a square peg in a round hole, but other times I'm lucky, like this evening; I meet someone I know, who's nice to talk to, like you.'

'You've boosted my confidence no end.'

'You don't need an extra boost. You look better than most of the other women here tonight, and I could tell yesterday that you can hold an intelligent conversation. That doesn't apply to most of them.' He looked around. 'The majority are only concerned about what brand of lipstick their rivals use.'

Rebecca's eyes sparkled. 'You are a lifesaver.

He smiled. She tucked her arm through his. 'Shall we simply study all the paintings, and find something atrocious to say about each one?'

His eyes twinkled and his mouth turned up. 'What a good idea!'

Rebecca deliberately avoided the others. Whenever she looked in their direction, they seemed to be standing in exactly the same positions. She wondered if any of them had bothered to look at a painting or one of the sculptures. The evening seemed to be a waste of their time.

Clive and she ate some of the titbits circling the room on ornate silver trays, and helped themselves to another drink. They made quiet insulting remarks about each of the paintings as they travelled around the room, although were kind enough to agree that some of them at least had a good choice of colours.

Eventually, he looked at his watch. 'Well, I've done my duty. I'm off!'

Rebecca was a little dismayed. 'I'd like to leave too. I have to wait until the others decide to go.'

'Would you like me to give you a lift home?'

The relief was evident. 'Really? That would be kind. Or I could take a taxi — if I can get someone to call me one.'

'Don't bother; it's more or less on my way. You're still staying with Mrs Barsetti?'

'Thank you! I'll just say goodbye.'

'Won't they mind — you leaving with me?'

'They'll probably be glad they don't have to take me home. Won't be long!'

'I'll get my car and see you outside.'

Rebecca nodded. 'I'll hurry.' She drew a deep breath and made her way through the throng to the Barsetti family.

Chiara smiled. 'Ah, there you are. I wondered where you were!'

Rebecca forced her lips into a stiff smile and tried to ignore Luca's presence. 'I was with Clive Oliver. We've examined all the paintings and the sculptures.'

'And? What do you think? Do you like anything? Imagine buying one of them?'

She had nothing to lose. 'No; I haven't got that sort of money, and I don't particularly like a single one either.'

Chiara's laugh pealed out and Marco nodded understandingly. Luca said nothing and Antonia looked rather disdainful.

Rebecca ploughed on: 'Clive is leaving, and he's offered me a lift home. I'm going, but I wanted to say thanks to Antonia for the invitation.' She gave Antonia a cursory look. 'And I wanted to thank you and Marco for picking me up.'

Chiara was secretly watching Luca's expression; he was standing opposite. His lips tightened and his eyes narrowed slightly. Chiara noticed he'd been studying the crowd ever since he arrived. She was sure he'd been surreptitiously watching Rebecca's progress around the pictures and sculpture on display. Chiara's mood improved noticeably. She said, 'Are you sure? We're thinking of going to a night-club for a drink!'

Rebecca shook her head. 'Thanks anyway. Thanks for everything!' She held out her hand to Chiara, Marco and Antonia. Antonia's smile was as limp as her hand. Rebecca offered Luca a brief nod and swallowed the lump in her throat. 'I'll see you tomorrow?' She didn't wait for his answer and turned away. Clive was waiting, and Rebecca was glad to escape.

11

Rebecca shared a leisurely breakfast with Luca's grandmother. She gave her the borrowed brooch back and asked her to return Chiara's dress for her.

In the sunlit dining room, Rose Barsetti said, 'Yes, of course I will. She calls regularly to see me.'

Rebecca repacked the small holdall. Luca was collecting her at twelve. She was nervous, so she went for a walk, and when she got back Luca was chatting with his grandmother. He was warm and charming with the elderly lady, and politely reserved with Rebecca, only muttering a quick 'Good morning'. His grandmother noticed, and was secretly amused. Rebecca wondered how the atmosphere would be when they were on their own. She thanked her hostess and gave her a gentle hug before she followed Luca to the car.

The same driver sat behind the wheel

as on Friday. He took her bag for the boot. She'd known she couldn't avoid Luca indefinitely; he was her boss. From the look on his face, she wondered if she'd be his secretary for much longer.

He opened the car door and she got in. He produced a piece of folded paper from the pocket of his navy-blue slacks. 'The dog is doing well. Here's the telephone number. You can check for yourself when we get back to San Andreas — that's if you want to.'

Colour flooded her cheeks temporarily. She hadn't forgotten the dog, but had expected the vet to contact her. She didn't even have the address. She accepted the note and put it quickly into her bag. 'Thanks. I'm glad. I wanted to phone your friend but I didn't know his number.'

He looked at her sceptically. 'No doubt you were too busy shopping to check the telephone directory. You brought the queries from Howell's? I'll go through them now.'

The remark about shopping was petty, but he was right. She'd insisted on rescuing the dog, but hadn't made much effort since then. She'd been too busy with her own problems. She bit her lip and her colour deepened. She said, 'Yes, they're in my overnight bag.'

He told the chauffeur to fetch Rebecca's holdall again. She ruffled through the contents. The papers were at the bottom, and various things spilled onto the car's carpeted floor. At last, she found them. He picked up a pair of cream panties, and dangled them from one finger. Rebecca thrust the papers at him with one hand and grabbed the lacy object with the other, colour flooding her face again. Shoving everything haphazardly into the bag, she didn't see the annoyance fade, and the humour return to his eyes. By the time she handed the chauffeur the bag again and settled into her seat, Luca was busy in the other corner with the papers.

She looked out of the window, and

hoped that he wouldn't want to talk. He didn't, but after a short time, she wished that he did. He concentrated on the paperwork, asked no questions, and made no comments.

Rebecca decided he was an infuriating, and absolutely fascinating, man. Her brain kept telling her not to think about him; but her heart didn't listen. Rebecca looked unseeingly at the passing scenery, and wondered how long she could function without making a fool of herself. They approached the ferries, but suddenly branched off along another side road that led to an area where expensive yachts were berthed in a sheltered harbour.

Luca shuffled the papers together, shoved them into his briefcase, and started to get out. He explained, 'I decided to sail back.' His eyes narrowed.

'And you want me to come with you?'

'The last ferry has already left. Sunday sailing times are different.

Unless you want to spend the night in the ferry port, you haven't much choice.'

There was room to walk around on the ferry, and they wouldn't be on their own. She swallowed a lump in her throat.

Without further ado, he took their bags from the chauffeur. Luca thanked him briskly; the man tipped his cap and withdrew. He preceded her along the quayside to a yacht berthed there. *Aphrodite* was small and beautiful, and she glistened in the bright sunshine as she bobbed in the water. He jumped aboard and held out his hand to help her. She took it and he released it as soon as she landed on the deck.

'Make yourself comfortable; take a look around. I use the engine to leave the port; it's quicker and safer. Can you sail?'

'No.'

'Pity! Then you'd better wear a lifejacket. I don't fancy recuing you if you fall in.'

'I promise not to do anything silly, and I can swim.'

He eyed her carefully. 'Well, as long as you're sensible, and the weather stays like this, it should be okay.' He jumped back onto the quay to untie the mooring lines, back again to rev the engine, and then manoeuvred the boat into rougher water beyond the harbour walls.

The engine hummed gently, and the boat rocked as they hit the open sea. It was exhilarating. The breeze whipped through her hair as they drew further away from the coastline. There were blue skies and white-crested green waves as they sailed out into the Gulf waters. After a while, he cut the engine, and ran up the main sail with electronic help. Even Rebecca could tell he was a skilled sailor.

'We have a couple of hours' sailing ahead of us. I have to sail around San Andrea to the private harbour on the other side.'

Rebecca nodded and sat down in the

comfortable upholstered seat behind the steering wheel. There was a protective awning overhead. He glanced in her direction. 'Any signs of seasickness?'

She shook her head. She decided to attempt normal conversation. 'No, it's okay. Being rich certainly does have its compensations, doesn't it?' She brushed strands of straying hair out of her eyes.

He looked more relaxed, and she hoped it meant there would be a better atmosphere between them. He was immersed in the task of controlling the boat. He clearly enjoyed sailing immensely.

Rebecca had time to secretly admire how his white knitted pullover clung neatly to his ample chest, and how the zipped-collar flapped wildly around his throat for a while until finally he closed it. They were images she wanted to commit to memory for later. She hugged herself tightly as the cool winds began to whip the warmth from her body. He noticed, extracted a navy-blue cabled sweater from below one of the seats, and wordlessly threw it across to her.

She smiled gratefully. 'Thanks.' She slid it over her head and inhaled the smell of him. The pullover was too long and too large, but she'd never felt better. Time flew as they sped across the ocean. There was only one other boat in sight, and that was a small black dot in the distance.

His voice cut in on her thoughts. 'Take the wheel for a minute.'

'That's not a good idea. I don't know what to do.'

'Do nothing, just hold position until I've lowered the sail and dropped anchor.'

Rebecca looked at the empty expanse of ocean where the blue-green waves were gently dancing in a never-ending rhythm. 'And then?'

'We make a short stop. I haven't had any breakfast. Can you cook?'

Rebecca swallowed quickly. 'It depends. I'm a secretary, not a cook.'

'Bacon and eggs? Or an omelette?'

Rebecca nodded and laughed softly. 'Yes, I can manage one of those.'

'Good. Now, come here!'

She took the wheel and concentrated on keeping it steady. He moved confidently, reeling in the sail from the aluminium mast and securing everything. He dropped anchor. 'There! Let's go below.'

He led the way and asked, 'Need any help in the galley?'

She shook her head and took off the sweater. She saw the expression as his eyes lingered on her body. She stroked her hair back into place, and her stomach knotted tightly.

The cabin was neat and decorated in navy blue. The small galley fridge was filled with fruit, eggs, cheese, bacon, milk and white wine. Some crusty bread was resting in a fixed basket on the wall. She searched for cooking utensils, and lit one of the gas burners. He flopped onto one of the seats curving around the table and watched her cracking eggs into a frying pan.

'Coffee?'

'Yes, please! The wine is tempting,

but sailing with a clear head is more important. You go ahead! Have some. Don't let me stop you.'

She turned back hurriedly to the stove and shook her head. 'No! Coffee will be fine for me too.'

A few minutes later, she piled savoury bacon and a couple of fried eggs onto a plate and handed it to him before edging herself in on the opposite side.

He waited patiently and looked pointedly. 'And? Where's yours?'

'I'm not hungry. I've already had breakfast.'

He stood up, tall and impressive, his hair nearly brushing the ceiling. 'Even you must be hungry again by now.' He scraped an egg and some of the bacon onto a fresh plate from the cupboard and put it in front of her. He also broke a chunk of bread off and handed it to her. 'Eat! That's an order.'

She smiled. 'I didn't need encouragement to eat anything eight years ago!' Rebecca dipped the fresh bread into the runny egg yolk and munched contentedly. It tasted good.

He rewarded her efforts with a smile. He was hungry, and there was a comfortable silence as he cleared his plate. She poured them coffee and sat down again. He cupped his hands around his mug.

'Would you like more?' she asked. 'There's still plenty of eggs and stuff in the fridge.'

Draining the mug and getting up to refill it, he shook his head. 'I'll have some fruit. What about you?

'Mmm! That's a very good idea.'

When he slipped back into place again with a bowl of fruit, she reached out for a handful of fat black grapes and he started to peel a peach.

Concentrating on his task, without looking at her, he asked, 'Why did you run away on Friday evening? Why did you prefer to go shopping with Chiara yesterday instead of visiting my house? And why did you prefer to spend the evening with that man instead of joining us? You can't pretend there's nothing fizzing between us, so why are you afraid of letting things take their course?' The peel curled in one piece as his knife cut its way through firm yellow flesh. It fell onto the plate and she stared at his long fingers, covered in juice.

She breathed deeply, and spoke honestly. 'You know why. I don't want to end up like all the rest.'

His eyes widened. 'What do you mean, 'all the rest'?'

She rose, and started to clear things away. Her legs were made of jelly. She had to put distance between them and avoid his face. 'I mean the all other women you've loved and left! I'm not passing judgement. You're entitled to live as you like, but I think differently about love and relationships. That's all!'

There was a tinge of irony in his voice. 'At least that means you are afraid something could happen, otherwise you wouldn't be so nervous. I was, and still am, a bachelor. Presumably you're referring to former affairs. You know how I felt about Antonia — that it was a mistake. Who are these 'other women'?'

Rebecca flushed and her answer came in a rush of words. 'Your name is continuously bandied about in the press, linked to lots of different women.'

He sounded ironic. 'I'm past thirty. It's not surprising that I've had the occasional girlfriend, is it?'

She was beginning to flounder. 'No — no, of course not — but . . . '

'And?' He waited.

She licked her lips. 'Well, there's all the stars and celebrities I've read about, Antonia for a start, and that woman you visited the other day. You looked like more than just friends.' She tried not to sound accusing. 'Your personal life is nothing to do with me, but I don't want to be available for a quick tumble between the sheets. I don't want to end up as another trophy.' She flushed and hurried on, 'There are plenty of socialites and others who will be delighted to share a meaningless affair. You don't need me.'

His expression was grim. 'Antonia? Yes, we went around for a while. You know that, I told you all about it! Our families thought it'd be perfect, but it was a big mistake. I thought it was about time to settle down. Antonia seemed to like me, and I knew it would make both families happy. I soon realized that would mean everyone would be — except me. Antonia and I come from different planets. Life with her would have been hell! After that, I gave up believing I'd fall in love one day.' He dragged his fingers impatiently through his hair, and Rebecca wondered if it now smelled of peach juice.

'Antonia still thinks she has rights to you, and she shows it.'

He shrugged. 'Antonia doesn't give up easily; that's one thing we do have in common, but there's not much else.'

Rebecca remained standing, her arms crossed defensively. 'Even if Antonia is passé, what about the woman you visited the other day? She was absolutely delighted to see you. I drew my own conclusions. How many more are there like her? Is there one in every port; in every town? I'm too straightforward for your world.' There was a swishing sound as the waves buffeted the yacht. She stared at him, her heart pounding erratically.

He glanced at her sharply. 'Women have always been part of my life; sometimes because I liked them, sometimes because they liked my money. Do you condemn me for that? Don't tell me you've never had a boyfriend; I wouldn't believe you. Not many people find the right person straight off.' He paused, thinking over her words. 'What do you mean about the woman the other day? What woman?'

She took a deep breath. 'The one you called to see when we were on the way from the ferry to your grandmother's.'

He looked puzzled for a moment, before he began to laugh. 'Rebecca!

That is funny enough to be sad. She's the widow of the pilot who was killed in the plane crash. I met her at the funeral, and I offered to sort out the paperwork. Our company insured him, and now she'll get enough financial support to make a decent life for herself and her daughter. It won't replace him, but it is the best we can do. She's a very nice, courageous woman.'

She paled. 'She was the pilot's wife? I presumed she was just another — !'

He came slowly to his feet, his eyes burning in his face. 'Well, you were wrong, weren't you? Give us a chance, Rebecca! Don't slam the door in my face; it took me eight years to realize how special you are, but I do now.' He closed the distance between them, and Rebecca's legs threatened to give way. He crushed her to him and pressed his lips on hers. She clung on to his neck and kissed him back, lingering and savouring every moment. Her mouth opened under his. She'd always been in love with him, and she didn't want to resist any more. She was past the point of no return; there was no room for sensible calculations or for pointless regrets.

His voice whispered in her hair as he pulled her closer to his body. 'Rebecca, trust me! We'd be very stupid to ignore what's happening. There's no guarantee for us; I can only tell you I've never known anyone who affects me like you do.'

Her voice was hoarse, and a mere whisper. 'I'm sorry I got things mixed up.' Their eyes met and merged.

'I need to know. Is there someone else, another adoring Peter Stanley, somewhere back home?' He waited in rigid silence, afraid in case she'd answer yes.

The atmosphere was electric; their breathing was harsh and uneven. The sheer nearness of his body sent shivers of delight through her body. 'No, there's no one.'

His smile flashed and transformed his face. 'This wasn't supposed to happen here.'

Rebecca felt a ripple of mirth emerging. 'Wasn't it? Then where — if I may ask?'

He gave a chuckle that swelled to loud and gleeful laughter. Rebecca couldn't help it; she joined in. He looked at her mischievously. 'I wanted you to visit my house. But you torpedoed that, didn't you?' She coloured. 'This yacht may not be quite as spacious, but it's infinitely more private.' He swept her into his arms, and his mouth captured hers as he shuffled her through the door of the adjoining cabin.

*　*　*

Rebecca guessed from the light coming through the porthole that it was late afternoon. Luca had covered her with a blanket before he left. He was a surprising man, utterly cold-blooded in some ways, but also very gentle and caring. The yacht was underway again. It was rocking gently and the water was slapping the keel as it cut through the water. She stretched contentedly and got up. She began to collect her clothes from where they'd been abandoned. She put on the dark-blue sweater again and locked her arms around herself, in the sheer joy of having something that was his. She tidied the cabin, and climbed the cabin steps. She was still unsure, because her thoughts were in utter disarray. Was she another sexual adventure, a challenge, another conquest? Now that she'd slept with him, perhaps his interest would fade.

He smiled when he saw her, and motioned her to him. 'Come here!'

Rebecca obeyed. He held the steering wheel with one hand and pulled her close with the other. She leaned back and felt contented and happy.

'I was just thinking of how well we've always understood each other. I wish I'd been clever enough to realize how special you were eight years ago.'

Rebecca smiled confidently and shook her head. 'There were too many other attractions. We were good friends, and that was enough for me in those days.'

'You were always a lovely person. You may have changed physically since then; but you are the same lovely person today.' He shrugged. 'I'm so grateful fate has given us a second chance. I need you, Rebecca; you're the other half of me that's always been missing.' He kissed the top of her head.

Rebecca wrapped her hands around the muscled arm that was holding her tight. Her heart was turning cartwheels. 'And where do we go from here? I'm still your secretary.'

'What do you mean?' He looked puzzled.

'I mean, we have to finish the book, and we're not alone on San Andrea.'

He spun her around, placed his hands back on the steering wheel, and formed a box where she could stand and face him. He looked at her and grinned. 'And? Where's the problem?'

She punched his chest playfully. 'You know what I mean. I'm talking about Giraldo and Franca.'

He eyed her speculatively. 'Don't tell me I have to keep my hands off you till after the book is finished. I won't listen!'

'Think about Franca and Giraldo, how they'll react if we go around like demented lovers.'

'Demented? I'm not demented! I've never felt so sane. Look! Let's take one step at a time! It might not be as complicated as you think.' He kissed the tip of her nose, her eyes, and then her mouth — so softly that she barely felt his lips brushing her skin, but the effect was purely sensual.

She was trying to hang on to reality but he made her senses reel. Brushing loose tendrils of her hair impatiently aside, she was unaware of how captivating she looked. 'Will you at least try to pretend whenever they're around; just to please me? I'd feel happier!'

His mouth dropped open, and he mumbled, 'I don't believe it! As long as they're around — they're around all the time!'

'No, they're not. How many times do you actually see them during the day? And once Franca serves the evening meal, and clears the kitchen, they both disappear for the day. I've never seen either of them on my side of the house once it gets dark.' She blushed a little as her voice faded to a quiver and she saw the sparkle in his eyes.

'Ah! Clandestine assignations. Do I need a disguise as well? Would you prefer Superman or Zorro?'

She punched his shoulder. 'Don't be silly! I'm trying to be sensible. I don't want Franca to think badly of me.'

He gave a deep sigh. 'Okay, okay! I don't understand why, but I'll try not to flaunt my infatuation. But just remember, the day we finish the book, I won't give a damn about what anyone else says or thinks anymore.'

Rebecca's heart leapfrogged. She stood on tiptoe and cradled his face in her hands, before she kissed him satisfyingly on the velvet warmth of his lips. 'Thanks, Luca.'

Recklessly, he let go of the wheel and reclaimed her with a kiss that left her breathless and longing for more. There was something between them that unlocked desire whenever they touched. She'd vowed not to get involved with him, but she was lost forever. He took her hand and kissed the palm before he turned his attention wholly to steering again.

He tried unsuccessfully to don a serious expression. 'If this yacht capsizes, we'll have a very long and tiring swim to shore. Will you make some coffee, please! If I hadn't already told Giraldo we'll be arriving this afternoon, I'd be tempted to sail on, and make love to you under the stars, but I'll save that for another day.'

'Promises! Promises!' She ducked under his arms and skipped across the sparse deck towards the cabin steps. Her cheeks were hot with happiness. She couldn't believe it. This was a moment never to forget; it wasn't the time to worry about the future.

Hours later, the yacht chugged gently

to its mooring place, and Luca cut the engine. He threw Giraldo the mooring lines. Rebecca sighed inwardly; the last couple of hours had been heaven. As far as she was concerned, the journey could have gone on for ever. He squeezed her hand as he helped her ashore and their eyes met silently.

Giraldo wiped his forehead with his red kerchief. 'Hello, Rebecca! Enjoy the trip? You've got lots of colour in your cheeks.'

'Hi, Giraldo! Yes, I've never been on a yacht before. It was unforgettable.'

He nodded and turned to Luca. 'The car is over there.' He eyed the yacht. 'It could do with a going-over; I'll come down and give it a wash tomorrow.'

Rebecca was glad she'd tidied the cabin before they arrived.

They crossed the road to the Jeep, and by the time Giraldo joined them, they were sitting demurely side-by-side in the back seat. Giraldo viewed them in his driving mirror, but they looked in opposite directions. What he couldn't see was that Luca was fingering her hand and that Rebecca's face was full of happiness. She already knew it was going to be very hard to disguise her love from other people.

She pirouetted when she was alone in the outhouse. After unpacking the holdall, she looked at her watch, then sat on the terrace with some juice and an unread paperback to wait impatiently to go across to the main house to see him again. Perhaps it was a silly idea to try to keep things from Giraldo and Franca, but her instincts told her not to broadcast her happiness. She knew that she couldn't stop loving him now, even if she tried; it was too late for that.

He grabbed her from behind the door as she came in for the evening meal, and the laughter bubbled up and fell from her lips. 'Be sensible.'

'I'm already regretting that I agreed to this stupid farce.'

He kissed her, and she gave in momentarily to the euphoria, before she slipped from his arms and took her usual place on the opposite side of the dining table. 'It's better not to draw attention to ourselves.'

He groaned and took his place at the table before shaking out his serviette and letting it fall onto his lap. 'This is utterly ridiculous. It's the twenty-first century.'

'And we're on San Andrea. We're in your family's house, being looked after by your employees. It would make them feel awkward. If we went around like two star-struck lovers, Franca would probably fetch the local priest to lecture us.'

There was a gentle knock and Franca opened the door. She carried a tray and smiled before she began to arrange various dishes in the centre of the table. Rebecca saw they'd be able to serve themselves. The entrée was already arranged on small plates: a cold Italian salad with cheeses, tomatoes and olives. Franca spoke to Luca rapidly in Italian. There was fish and rice for the main course; it was hot and waiting in the dish. She put the dessert on the side table with a thermos jug of coffee.

'Do you wish me to serve, Mr Barsetti, or will you serve yourselves?'

He replied in English: 'No, that's not necessary, Franca. We'll serve ourselves. Why don't you have an early night? I'm sure Rebecca will pile the dishes on the tray and carry them to the kitchen when we're finished, won't you, Rebecca?'

'What?' She felt his foot kick hers softly under the table, and she looked across to read the message in his eyes. 'Oh, yes! Yes, of course. No trouble!'

Franca nodded. 'Goodnight Rebecca; goodnight Mr Barsetti!'

The door closed quietly behind her and they looked at each other for a few seconds, until Franca was out of ear-shot. Rebecca burst into laughter. 'That is not the way to stop her curiosity.'

'Perhaps not, but I've got you to myself. I don't think she'll come back now without a very good reason.'

'I'm hungry.'

'So am I, but not just for food.' His eyes sparkled as he half-rose and reached across the table for her hand. Rebecca ran her fingers down the side of his face; he kissed the inside of her wrist gently before he took her hand between his and gave a wicked grin. 'Right; let's eat first, and concentrate on the rest afterwards!'

12

His head materialized round the door with a look that made Rebecca feel good to be alive. He strode towards the desk and picked up her hand. He smiled quickly. 'You'll notice I'm remembering our game of hide and seek! I made sure Franca or Giraldo weren't up here before I came.' He paused. He knew Rebecca didn't want to hear what he had to say next. 'Please, don't get annoyed, but Antonia has just phoned to ask if she can come for a meal this evening.'

Her heart plummeted. 'Oh!' She bit her lip and tried to look unconcerned. Her heartbeat skyrocketed again as he pulled her to her feet and enclosed her in his arms. Stroking her hair with his hand, he said, 'I promise that there's not the slightest reason for you to get annoyed. She won't ever come between us, I swear! If we trust one another, no one can.'

Rebecca was reassured that he could read her mind.

'I know you don't like her, but please try to understand. I can't ignore her completely; our families have known each other too long.' He hooked his finger under her chin and lifted her face so that he could look into her eyes. 'Try to be generous; we've got what she's never had, and probably never will!'

She swallowed hard and nodded. 'How long will she stay?'

'She isn't staying. She suggested doing a shooting session here for an American magazine. She asked if she could bring the photographer and owner of the magazine for a meal before they leave.'

Her worries lessened. 'She's leaving after the meal?'

He nodded. 'I gather there's a helicopter pick-up as part and parcel of the arrangement. The rest of the team come, and leave, with the ferry. Antonia and these two men will leave following the evening meal. But if you feel you can't face her . . . '

'I can't pretend I like her and I'm not sorry she isn't to be staying, but I'll try to be agreeable.'

He gave her a smile and a swift kiss. 'Exactly as I hoped! I'd better tell Franca, before I forget. I'll leave you to your work now, although I'm tempted to order you to join me in a more interesting pastime.'

The depth of his suggestive smile excited her. 'That's certainly not how to finish this book. I don't mind staying away this evening if it makes things easier.'

'Oh, Rebecca! Of course I want you there! I'm sure she already senses you mean more to me that she ever did. You might not believe it, but Antonia can be charming when she tries, and I'm hoping she accepts the situation and behaves herself.'

'I'll keep my fingers crossed.'

He slipped his hand round her waist.

'How's the work coming along?'

'I've almost finished typing the last chapters. You can have them tomorrow morning. I'm putting in the new corrections and copying the chart about market fluctuations.'

He picked up the hand-drawn chart and studied it carefully. 'Bold italics for the title, and capital letter for this section, so that they see what's important at a glance.' Rebecca studied him. 'Don't split the sentence there, like I have. It distracts.'

She freed herself, and made notes on the chart. He bent to kiss her forehead and smiled again. Her insides did somersaults as his finger skimmed the side of her jawbone, and he kissed her on her lips quite satisfyingly before he headed for the door.

Rebecca took special care with her looks that evening. She couldn't compare with Antonia's striking appearance, but she'd learned how to make the best out of her features. When she entered the dining room, the others were already sipping aperitifs. She saw the admiration and love in Luca's eyes as she walked towards where they were gathered. Rebecca knew nothing could spoil the evening for her as long as he was there. Antonia noticed too, but apart from her fingers tightening on the stem of her glass, she gave nothing away.

To Rebecca's surprise, Antonia was making an effort to be charming. There was no comparison with the cynical, derisive woman she'd known previously. Luca eyed Antonia suspiciously through narrow eyes. The other two men were content that Antonia was being nice. Most top photo models were moody and difficult, and Antonia was no exception. Tonight, though, Antonia was all sugar and spice.

The meal went well, and Rebecca had to admit that Antonia contributed intelligently to the conversation and didn't torpedo anyone else's views. Topics were general; everyone could join in. Antonia didn't even bat an eyelid when they spoke English all the time. The chill didn't leave her eyes when she looked at Rebecca; but apart from that, Rebecca couldn't fault her.

Deep in thought, Rebecca jumped when Antonia addressed her. 'Did you enjoy the dinner-party?'

'Yes. Did you?'

Antonia dabbed the corner of her mouth delicately with her serviette. 'Of course. It's a good to be with the family and meet friends and acquaintances, isn't it, Luca?' Luca didn't answer. She held her wine glass for him to fill. He obliged politely. 'Did you know that your grandmother has mislaid her pearl necklace?'

Luca wasn't very interested, but could hardly ignore the remark. 'Really! No, I didn't.'

'The beautiful one with the black pearls.' She smiled.

Rebecca looked at Antonia, her knife and fork poised in mid-air. 'How awful! I hope she finds it soon. Things like that worry old people a lot.'

Antonia shrugged. 'Yes, a valuable

snuffbox is missing too. They only noticed it yesterday. The last I heard, they were still searching and hoping it was just mislaid in the general clean up after the party. Maria says she remembered seeing the necklace on the dressing table on Saturday morning, but your grandmother can't even remember that!'

'She often forgets where she puts things. I remember she lost a pair of earrings once, and Marco and I combed every inch of the garden searching for them because she was certain she'd lost them there. In the end, they found them in the kitchen on the windowsill. No one had noticed them for days.'

Antonia smothered a yawn with her slender hand. She turned to Rebecca again. 'I'd hate to lose any of my jewellery, wouldn't you?'

Rebecca smiled. 'I don't own much, and nothing of great value.'

Antonia studied her manicured nails. 'What's for dessert? I shouldn't indulge, really. I'll have to work off all these extra calories tomorrow.'

Luca rang the bell. Franca came to collect the dishes and serve the créme caramel. Luca asked the men about their jobs and Antonia added some interesting additions. Rebecca was amazed by Antonia's friendliness.

Two hours later, the sound of rotor blades cutting through the air brought the evening to an end. The photographer shouldered his precious cameras; he didn't allow anyone else to handle them. Both men thanked Luca for his hospitality and said goodnight to Rebecca. Rebecca said goodbye, and Antonia and the two men followed Luca out to the landing platform in a field beyond the house.

The helicopter was waiting. The rotor blades spun, the engine roared loudly as it took off, and the machine headed out over the sea towards the mainland. A glance out of her bedroom window showed Rebecca its flashing red lights fading into the distance.

She began to get ready for the night.

The sound of the door opening and closing downstairs sent her senses spiralling. She stood expectantly, listening to his steps hurrying up the stairs. Her breath caught in her throat as they faced each other in the dim light of the bedroom.

★ ★ ★

'This is farcical.' The dawn was breaking and Luca was dressing.

There was a mischievous look in her eyes as she leaned back into the pillow and watched the muscles in his back ripple. She said, 'No it's not. You are protecting my reputation.'

'My lovely Rebecca, I'm ruining it!' Luca turned to her, his dark eyes riveted on her face and body. He leaned forward and kissed her gently.

She stared at his expression, and wished the moment would never end. He was silent; then he whispered, 'You realise there's no turning back for us, don't you?' He watched her, his gaze wandered over her face, and the tips of his fingers brushed the surface of her lips.

Rebecca replied softly, 'Yes, I know.'

He rose quickly and turned; his voice sounded normal again. 'Coffee?'

She smiled gratefully. 'No, thanks. I'll laze, and think about us.'

'That's a very worthwhile pastime!' He kissed her quickly again on her forehead. 'If I'm going, it had better be now, otherwise I'll — ' His finger trailed across her bare shoulder. 'I'll go for my usual swim, and continue to hide the truth from Franca. I still think all this is very stupid. We're adults; I don't mind who knows.' He crossed the room towards the open staircase quickly, and turned briefly to look at her again before he disappeared.

Rebecca stared at the ceiling. The sunrise was sending splashes of gold through the windows. For a few seconds the walls were shades of honey and jonquil. She didn't know why, but the expression 'fool's gold' came to mind. Was she living in a fool's paradise?

She turned her head and thumped the pillow. Luca did care! She could tell he did, but how much? She'd read too much about his various affairs to feel entirely secure yet. Impatiently, she tried to ignore her negative thoughts; but the question of why Luca Barsetti would want someone as insignificant as Rebecca Summer was always at the back of her mind.

Perhaps she shouldn't expect too much too soon. They'd only just begun to get to know each other properly. Neither of them actually knew if their feelings would stand the test of time.

She sat up and encircled her knees with her arms; the sheets fell away, and soon the cool morning air spread a chilled layer across her skin. She was reminded of the warmth of his body, and she wished he was here. Throwing back the duvet, she got up and donned her running gear. By the time she'd got back and had breakfast, she actually managed to think of work again.

The knowledge that he might come into the office at any minute added a new excitement to her day. She made steady progress and tried not to be distracted. She concentrated on inserting corrections and solving queries. She loved him, and longed to sit and dream, but she didn't — not in working hours. Her quiet, desperate attempts to keep him at arm's length in the office amused him. When the day's work ended, they usually met on the beach, where they held long discussions lying on rugs in the sunshine. They could make love hidden from view as if they were the only people on earth. They met again for the evening meal, so they were spending nearly all day together in one way or another. Rebecca had never felt happier in her life. Just looking at him sent her senses haywire.

This morning, she looked across the room as the door opened; he paused when he came inside. Rebecca smiled automatically, but the smile faded when she noted the expression on his face. 'Is something wrong?'

His expression was grim.

'Luca, something is wrong, isn't it? Your parents? Your grandmother?'

He stood stiffly and answered with desperate firmness, 'You remember Antonia saying that my grandmother lost a necklace?'

She nodded wordlessly; the lack of warmth in his eyes hit her like a jet of cold water. 'A pearl necklace. Black pearls.'

'Franca cleans this place once a week.'

Rebecca nodded. 'And?' She waited.

'Today, when she was emptying the towels from the laundry basket in the bathroom, she found these wrapped in a cloth at the bottom.' He drew a gold snuffbox out of his pocket, and a string of black pearls.

A quick intake of shocked breath filled her lungs. She stared in utter astonishment. 'Your grandmother's necklace? But how on earth . . . ?'

His eyes were expressionless, dark and unfathomable. 'That's what I'd like to know. Do you know anything about it?'

'Do I know . . . ?' She opened her mouth and shut it again. For a second she was too stunned to react as one bewildered thought outpaced the next. 'Luca what are you suggesting?' Her stomach was knotted and the pitch of her voice rose. 'Are you accusing me of stealing your grandmother's necklace?'

The tense lines on his face deepened; his voice was cool and controlled. 'I'm not accusing you of anything. I'm only asking if you have a logical explanation about how this necklace got into your laundry basket?'

'No, I haven't.' She clenched her nails until they cut into the palms of her hands and the colour drained from her face. Her voice sounded as shaky as she felt. 'I haven't seen the necklace before.'

He rewrapped the necklace in his handkerchief, slipped both things back into his pocket, and nodded. 'I had to ask you. You understand?'

She stiffened and swallowed hard. At the back of her eyes tears of disbelief were forming. 'No, I don't. I thought you trusted me, but you don't, do you? I can't believe you think I'm involved.' Her tone hardened. 'But perhaps I'm the perfect culprit: a temporary secretary, with an average income. Perhaps you ought to ask me if I gave your gran the brooch back which she lent me for the art exhibition, too? Perhaps I'm someone who steals jewellery from an old lady!'

His expression was stiff and cold. 'Oh, stop being so dramatic, Rebecca. You're talking rubbish. Instead, just tell me how you think the necklace could have got here.'

She felt bitter, and her voice had an ominous quality. 'I have no idea! I've just told you so.' Something shot through her brain, but she held her tongue. Antonia would do anything, absolutely anything, to get him back. Antonia's recent visit had something to do with it, but he had to figure that out for himself. If she said something, he'd just put it down to spite.

He looked puzzled and ran his hand through his hair. 'Maria said she thinks she saw the necklace on Saturday morning, the day after the party.'

Rebecca's eyes were stony, and sarcasm spilled into her voice. 'Then that ties it up nicely, doesn't it? I was there on Saturday until Sunday lunchtime, wasn't I? It fits perfectly!' She turned away abruptly. His mistrust rankled immensely. 'There's no point in continuing this conversation, is there? I'm clearly your number-one suspect!'

He'd bungled it. Luca understood her anger, and wondered how he could reassure her. He only wanted to collect facts, and ask what she thought about it; but somehow it had backfired. She felt under attack, and he had to defuse the situation fast. When Franca gave him the necklace, he'd gone automatically to Rebecca. He'd thought she'd have sensible suggestions. He didn't reckon that his remarks would sound like accusations. He knew Rebecca would never steal anything. Admittedly, his phrasing was bad, and he probably did sound as if he was condemning her.

'I'm not accusing you, Rebecca, but I have to get to the bottom of it, surely you understand that? I can't ignore it. I can't pretend a valuable necklace has travelled magically across the sea to your laundry basket. What do you expect me to do?'

Her face was white. She lowered her glance, and started to fidget with some papers on the desk. Her lashes fanned across her cheeks. She was usually pale, but at the moment, she was deathly white. She didn't know what she was doing, and she certainly wasn't able to think rationally. His words were poison. If he doubted her the least bit, he definitely didn't love her after all.

With a lump in her throat, she replied, 'Find the thief. I repeat, I did not steal that necklace, and I have no idea how it got into my bathroom. If you'll excuse me, I want to finish this before lunch.' Her voice was frosty. 'If I can do anything to help, please don't hesitate to ask.'

Not used to backing down, or admitting that he'd bungled things, Luca looked for a quick and easy loophole. 'I'm going to phone my grandmother to reassure her, and then I intend to get some professional advice about what to do.' He lifted his hand in a gesture of conciliation. 'Don't put up any barricades, Rebecca!'

A thought crossed her mind. 'Have you questioned Giraldo or Franca about it?'

He looked uncomfortable. 'No. I trust them. They're not involved.'

She stiffened. 'I thought as much.' She ploughed on. 'May I remind you, anyone could have got into the outhouse in my absence? You know the door is never locked. It seems I'm the only one who needs questioning.' She fiddled with the computer keyboard. 'You'd better phone your grandmother; I'm sure she'll be glad to hear the necklace is safe.'

Luca had never had to cope with anything similar. Rebecca was reacting like a child, but he understood why. He had to put things right. 'I'm only trying to figure out the most sensible way to handle this.'

She tried to look unconcerned. 'Good! Then carry on!' She turned away, pretending to search for a folder in the filing cabinet. Tears were at the back of her eyes, but she was determined he wouldn't see them. She took a deep breath and ignored the knot tightening in her chest. Flipping through papers, she carried on pretending to search for something she didn't need.

He wanted to kiss some sense into her brain. Why was she so obstinate? Did she want him to fall to his knees and apologise; did she just want to hear that she had complete power over him, body and soul? He grumbled under his breath in Italian before he turned without another word and closed door with a bang as he ran headlong down the stairs.

Rebecca stared at the door. She waited a couple of seconds for him to move out of hearing then she swept the typewritten sheets and various other items angrily from the desk; they scattered all over the floor. It didn't help. She'd only made more work for herself. She'd now have to retype every damaged page again. At least it made her concentrate on what she was doing and stopped her crying all the time.

Sounds of voices and doors opening and shutting heralded unusual happenings downstairs, but she ignored it and concentrated harder on finishing what she'd begun. She heard Luca's BMW roaring up the track, but resisted the urge to run to the window.

Coming downstairs, she met Franca.

Franca noticed her red-rimmed eyes and was upset. 'I'm sorry. I didn't know what to do. I met Mr Barsetti straight after I found the necklace and the box. I showed it to him. I didn't have a chance to talk you first.'

Rebecca reassured her: 'It's all right,

Franca. You did the right thing. What else could you do? I don't know how it got there. You know that it belongs to Mr Barsetti's grandmother?'

Franca nodded and bit her lip. 'He told me. He's very angry, and he spoke with the mainland for a long time on the phone. He told Giraldo he's going to the police.' She fumbled in her pocket. 'He asked me to give you this.'

Rebecca took the envelope and patted Franca on the shoulder. 'Don't worry. Oh, if Mr Barsetti isn't here, I'll make myself something to eat this evening.'

Almost affronted, Franca said. 'But I've already prepared some soup!'

Rebecca felt sick at the thought of food, but she signalled her agreement. 'Alright, I'll come across for some later, but don't make anything else.'

As soon as she was inside her lodgings, she closed the door and opened his note.

Rebecca,
An old schoolfriend of mine is a

criminal inspector in Taranto and I'm going to see him. I don't want to cross swords with you, and I intend to sort this problem out as fast as I can. I hope we'll then be able to talk things through quietly and sensibly again.

Carry on doing what you can as far as work is concerned. I'll be back soon.

Luca.

There was no 'Dear Rebecca', and no endearment at the end either. She felt shattered. She'd expected too much, given too freely of herself, and now had to accept the price she must pay.

13

Rebecca couldn't sleep. She loved Luca, and would never stop loving him, but she told herself that things would have probably gone haywire between them anyway. Luca was used to his freedom. Even if the theft of the necklace hadn't happened, they would have clashed because she didn't intend to give up the agency, not even for him. She wouldn't be happy frittering away her time like Chiara, with people who lived a kind of life she didn't understand. Being perfectly honest, she also admitted that he'd never even suggested that he wanted a permanent relationship.

She had to get on with her life without him again. She'd come to San Andrea with the intention of forgetting him, but she hadn't succeeded, and now she never would. Admittedly, the last few days had been wonderful: they were memories for evermore, all she'd ever have. She'd pay dearly for loving someone who didn't love her.

The book was almost ready. The last chapters were almost complete. She had corrections to make, and a pile of queries to clear up, but if she tried, all of that would only take a couple of days. If she was lucky, and the police had no objection, she could then leave. She presumed she'd have to face the police.

She spent Friday morning solving a handful of queries with a banking concern in Switzerland. After that, she was free to go through the book with a fine-tooth comb to see if she could find any other errors. She aimed to finish by the beginning of the coming week. Luca hadn't been in touch.

She was busy checking the layout of one of the charts when Franca knocked at the office door and came in. 'Rebecca, there's a policeman downstairs. He wants to talk to you.' Franca didn't like policeman; she looked worried and nervous.

Rebecca felt nervous too, although she knew she was innocent. She pushed back her chair and stood up. She straightened her skirt and followed Franca downstairs. There was a tall dark man waiting in the hall.

He held out his hand. 'Ah! Good morning! You are Miss Summer?' His eyes were sympathetic, and Rebecca relaxed a little.

'Yes. Good morning.'

'I'm Franco Barrissa.' He extracted his identification from his breast pocket and held it up for Rebecca to take a perfunctory glance. She saw that the picture matched his appearance. 'I'm with the local police. I expect you realise I've come to ask about the theft of Mrs Barsetti's necklace.'

'Yes. How can I help?'

'Luca — Mr Barsetti — reported what happened, and told us where the necklace was found. If you don't mind, I'd like to take a look?'

Rebecca nodded. 'No, of course not.'

He extracted a notebook and pen from his breast pocket. 'Miss Summer, I have to ask these questions, but please don't worry. If you were the thief, I'm sure you wouldn't have been stupid enough to leave the necklace in such an obvious place. A laundry basket that is emptied by the housekeeper at regular intervals is hardly the ideal spot. Anywhere else would have been more usual.'

Rebecca relaxed a little.

'We haven't yet figured out why it was put there, or who put it there, but we will. I have to ask these questions, it's routine. Can you imagine how the necklace came to be in your room?'

Rebecca locked her hands nervously. 'No, absolutely no idea.' She had no intention of mentioning Antonia. The agency might face a charge of slander if she did. It wasn't her job to solve the crime.

'Will you show me where it was found?'

'Follow me, please.' She took him across to the outhouse, was glad of the brief respite from questioning. There was a comforting breeze blowing in from the sea. He made small talk about the house and the island and she led him up the staircase into the bathroom. She pointed to the laundry basket standing against the wall, next to the shower.

'As far as I know, Franca found it at the bottom, underneath the dirty washing. I'm not sure if she takes the dirty washing from here across to the laundry, or if she collects the basket and empties it over there — she can tell you that herself.'

He crossed the room and lifted the lid, as if he expected a solution to pop up and hit him in the eye. 'Hmm! Mr Barsetti told me you don't lock the door?'

'Not during the day. As far as I know, none of the doors are locked during the day. We're a fair distance from the road, and someone would notice any stranger wandering around.'

He nodded. 'Luca said the same. But it is always better to lock a building if it's unoccupied.' He took his notebook out again. 'If you don't mind, I need some personal details. It won't take long.'

'Would you like some coffee or tea?'

'Coffee, please! I drink too much coffee, but my mind doesn't function without it anymore.' He smiled, and gestured for her to precede him downstairs again.

Rebecca made him coffee. He noted her name, address, and passport number, and she gave him a business card with telephone numbers and email addresses. He drained his mug and stood up.

'That was it! Thanks for the coffee and your cooperation.' He looked at his watch. 'I'll have a word with the house-keeper, and I might even be in time to catch the afternoon ferry.'

'It seems a long journey just to ask a couple of questions!'

He nodded. 'Perhaps. Normally, the local police would handle it, but there are no official police on the island. I know Luca and his grandmother very well.'

Luca and his family seemed to have connections wherever they went. 'I hope you find the thief soon. Made any progress?'

'One or two leads, but it's too early to say anything definite.'

'I . . . I was planning to go back to London at the beginning of next week. Is that alright? I'm just a temporary secretary here, and my work is almost finished. Do I have to stay until the case is solved?'

'No, you're perfectly free to travel. Luca wanted me to emphasise that you are free to do what you like. There is no shadow hanging over your head. If there are any more questions, I know where you are, either here or in London. Luca didn't say you were leaving . . . but if you are a temporary secretary, you can't wait forever, can you?' He looked at his watch. 'Will you show me where I can find Franca?'

On the way back to the main house, they chatted about the British police force. He seemed to be very knowledgeable; he knew more facts about how it functioned than Rebecca did. At the kitchen door, they shook hands, and she left him with Franca. On her way back to the outhouse, she thought about how he said she was free to go home; and she would. At least he'd given her a feeling she wasn't his prime suspect. But she had to clear up some things first.

'Hello, Mrs Barsetti, this is Rebecca.'

'Rebecca! How nice to hear from you!'

'Have you recovered from your lovely dinner-party?'

'Yes, it was enjoyable, wasn't it? I was tired after but it was worth it. Losing my necklace upset me, but I've got it back again now.'

'I understand why you're glad about that.'

'It's not just because it's valuable. I like it very much; I'd hate to lose it. I was amazed when Luca told me it turned up in your laundry basket.'

Rebecca paused. 'So was I! That's why I'm phoning, I wanted to tell you I honestly don't know how it got there.'

'Oh, of course not! If you'd stolen it, you wouldn't have been stupid enough to leave it in your room. You're too intelligent for that. It looks like someone wanted to put the blame on you, doesn't it? But it was a very stupid plan, if you ask me. I don't really care who did it, but Luca is determined to find out, and once he gets his teeth into something, he doesn't let go.'

A ton of bricks fell from her heart; she'd been worried in case his grand-mother thought badly of her. 'The police came here yesterday, but I couldn't help much.'

'They came to question me too. I suppose they have to follow procedures, and if the necklace showed up on San Andrea, then they have to go to San Andrea. I hope they find whoever did it soon, so that things settle down again.'

'So do I!'

'I suppose Luca is right when he says we have to find who did it, because they might try again. Enough about the necklace! How are you?'

'I'm fine, but there is a special reason for my call. I hope you can help me by doing me a big favour.'

'If I can, of course! Fire away! What is it?'

'Remember the dog I rescued?'

'The one I said I'd take, until you could sort things out? Yes.'

'I've just rung the vet, and found out that Dusty — that's what I've called him — is doing well. He broke a back leg, and it's still in plaster, but he's much better. Apparently he's ruling the roost and they're spoiling him dreadfully.'

Mrs Barsetti gave a tinkling laugh. 'Sound likes a great dog.'

'I — I'm leaving in a day or so, to go home. Are you still prepared to take Dusty until I can sort out the formalities and bring him into the UK?

The vet says he can keep him until the plaster comes off, but it would be wonderful if you could care for him after that? I can't settle things overnight, but I'll try to sort things out as soon as I can. If I can't keep him, I'm sure my mum will take him. It would be wonderful if you could look after him until I solve things.'

Rose Barsetti was startled. 'You're going? Going home? Luca didn't mention that.'

She swallowed hard and sounded unconcerned. 'He's busy at the moment, and probably forgotten that the book is more or less finished. There's no reason for me to stay; every extra day costs Luca money.' She laughed feebly.

'Does he know that you're going?'

Rebecca's voice faltered. 'I don't know where he is to tell him, and I'm sure he won't object. The sooner I get back to London, the sooner I can start to look for a new job.'

'It's none of my business, Rebecca, but wouldn't it be better to talk to him first?'

'Luca is a businessman; he won't want to waste money. It'd be silly to sit around twiddling my thumbs waiting for him to come back. He can contact me by phone, fax, or email if he needs more information, but that's not very likely. He has to pick out photos for the book, but he can do that on his own.'

'Well, I . . . '

Rebecca didn't want to talk about Luca. 'Dusty?' Rebecca's voice was begging.

'Oh, don't worry about Dusty; he can come as soon as the clinic lets him.'

Rebecca sighed with relief. 'He's already had all the various vaccinations, and the vet promised he'd find someone to bring him to you.'

'Then he can come straight away, with or without the plaster. It will save you kennel fees. I'll send someone to fetch him. Hang on a minute, give me the phone number and address.' She noted down the details.

'Oh, I'm so grateful; that's a weight off my mind! Dusty doesn't realise how lucky he is. I'll try to find a permanent solution as soon as possible.'

'Dusty was lucky that you found him in the first place. If you hadn't come along, he might be dead by now. I'll send you photos so that you can see how he's progressing. You must come back and see him, too.'

Rebecca didn't want to come back, although she felt real affection for Luca's grandmother. 'I'm relieved now I know that Dusty will be okay for a while, I'll try to get a flight home as soon as possible.'

Mrs Barsetti asked, 'How soon is soon?'

'Tomorrow, if I'm lucky! As soon as I find out about how I can get Dusty back to the UK, I'll let you know. The vet promised to help settle any formalities at this end, so I hope Dusty won't be a burden for too long.'

'Don't worry. If Dusty and I get on, I may not want to let him go.' Mrs Barsetti gave a chuckle. 'He's used to sunshine and warm temperatures. I don't think he'd be happy to exchange the sun for the cold and rain.'

'Oh, I hadn't thought about that. But he's my responsibility, and he might be too boisterous, or mischievous, or have bad habits; you may not want to keep him.'

' Keep in touch. You have my address and number? We'll settle Dusty's future between us.'

'Thank you so much, Mrs Barsetti.'

'My pleasure. Glad to help. Sorry you're leaving. How about making a detour to see me before you leave?'

'That's kind of you, but I want to get home as soon as possible. I've a living to make, and have to find myself another job as soon as possible.'

'I understand, but we'll see each other again, I'm sure.'

'I hope so. Oh, by the way, I've told the clinic to send me the bill for his treatment, so don't pay anything if they send you one by mistake.'

'Have a safe journey, Rebecca. Now that I know he's coming here, I'm looking forward to having your Dusty. Something to do; someone to care for!'

'Dusty is a lucky dog. Take care of yourself, Mrs Barsetti. Bye!'

'Bye, Rebecca!'

Rose Barsetti picked up the telephone and punched in another number.

Luca's housekeeper answered. 'Mr Barsetti? He's not here.'

'Oh! Where is he?'

'I don't know.'

'Is he in town somewhere?'

'I'm sorry, but I have no idea. He comes and goes. I'm not always here. Can I take a message?'

'Yes, leave him a message to tell him to phone me. It's very important.'

'I will.'

She rang Marco at company headquarters.

'Hello, Grandma! This is a surprise.'

'Marco, where's Luca?'

'I haven't a clue. Why?'

'I want to talk to him urgently, and no one seems to know where he is.'

'Is it that important?'

'Would I phone if it wasn't?'

'Sorry, stupid thing to say, wasn't it? No idea where he is. I saw him yesterday afternoon; he called in to sign some contracts. He had a meeting with someone from the police; something to do with your necklace, I think. Tried his mobile phone?'

'That blasted necklace! I've tried his phone, but there's no answer. It's switched off, or the battery's run out.'

'You sound worried. Can I help?'

'No thanks. It's something only Luca can handle — to do with Rebecca.'

'Ah! I see! If I see him, I'll tell him to phone you straight away.'

'Do that. Love to Chiara and the children.'

'I'll tell them!'

'Bye, Marco! I hope I haven't interrupted anything important?'

'Nothing in this company has ever been more important than Rose Barsetti.'

She chuckled. 'Oh, go on! You can flatter like your grandfather did. Bye!'

'Bye, Gran!'

She wondered what else she could do. She could only wait until Luca phoned her. No one knew where he was. She shrugged her shoulders in frustration, and picked up the paper with the vet's telephone number.

* * *

Less than an hour ago, Rebecca had said goodbye to Franca with a parting hug. They hadn't questioned why she was leaving. Why should they? There were constant visitors to the house who came and went.

Giraldo said, 'If you ever want to come back for a holiday, we'll find you somewhere to stay with one of our friends. You don't need an expensive boarding house. Just write, or phone, and we'll organise something. Come back when the wild flowers are in bloom, that's the best time of all.'

'Thanks.' Rebecca didn't intend to come back, ever. San Andrea was Luca, and she wanted to forget him, even though she already knew it'd be impossible. Her future stretched ahead in an endless string of futile dreams. She smiled at them both. 'Thank you for all your help and kindness.' Franca brushed her thanks aside as she got into the Jeep.

Rebecca was leaving, moving to a new stage in her life, away from a situation that had become unbearable. Leaving the small cottages, the narrow paths winding all over the little island, and the scents that belonged to another world. She leaned over the railing and waved to Giraldo for the last time. To her surprise, he was still among the crowd on the quay below, waiting for the ferry to depart. He lifted his hand as the ferry signalled its departure. It glided slowly out of the harbour, and soon he was just a small dark figure hurrying along the quay towards the Jeep parked in one of the side streets.

Rebecca remained at the ship's railing until the small island was a grey-green dot in the distance. She tried to store the memory of the sea, the blazing sun, and the tiny fleck of land in the ocean that she'd grown to love because Luca loved it. Finally, when it was just a tiny dot on the horizon, she turned away and concentrated on the mainland. Only a few weeks had passed, and so much had happened. She sat in lonely silence; felt drained and lifeless. A kind of permanent pain surrounded her as she realised that she'd never see him again.

She caught the train to Brindisi, and took a taxi to the airport. Once she was in the airport, she hurried through the formalities of Departures and looked for somewhere to wait for the boarding call. She looked at the face of her wristwatch. If they were on time, take-off was in three-quarters of an hour.

Rebecca read her newspaper, leaned back into one of the comfortable seats in the departure lounge, and forced herself to concentrate on the main articles. She hadn't read a newspaper for a couple of weeks, and time had moved on and left her standing. There were articles about world politics that were new to her. Her mobile phone rang. Who on earth? Jennifer? Her mother? She rummaged through her bag until she found it.

'Hello!'

'Rebecca?'

She jumped at the sound of his voice and bit her lips in dismay. 'Yes.' She managed to answer without falling apart.

'Where are you?'

Recovering from the surprise, she answered him calmly. 'At Brindisi airport.'

Silence reigned for a second. 'The airport? What the hell are you doing there?'

'I'm just about to board the plane. I'm going home.'

'And what about the book?'

He was worried about the book? Inwardly, she sighed with relief, but it was mixed with disappointment. She'd been right, she wasn't important. 'The book is finished. Everything is on my desk, including safety copies, and print-outs of anything I've changed since you left. I've done all I can do. The photos are your concern. I packed my bags and booked my ticket.'

He sounded in a bad temper. 'Who gave you permission to leave?'

Her hand clenched the mobile even tighter. 'Permission? You paid the agency for me to do a job. Four to five weeks was the agreement. The work was finished within that time, so why do I need permission?' She couldn't stop herself. 'You should be glad! I'm saving you money.'

He was shouting. 'I decide when the job is ended, not you. Turn around and go back to San Andrea.'

His tone sparked her anger. 'No, I will not! There is no reason for me to waste any more time for an official leave-taking.' Her voice dropped a tone, and she tried desperately to sound efficient. 'Perhaps you don't understand; there is nothing for me to do! I have a living to make. I need to look for a new job.'

A man in a business suit, sitting nearby, listened with interest. His curiosity irritated Rebecca; she turned her back, trying to compose herself and keep her voice under control.

His voice was cold, and had an ominous quality. 'The contract states that you will be available until I declare an end to our working relationship.'

Rebecca tried desperately to remember the exact wording; she couldn't. 'Does it? It's not in your interest or mine to unnecessarily prolong a contract. That's utterly ridiculous!'

'I need you to handle any modifications or amendments.'

She chose to ignore the undercurrents, and replied tersely, 'No, you don't. You can do that yourself now your hand is better. You don't need me.'

His voice dropped a little, and now had a steel edge to it. 'Rebecca, do you realise I can sue your agency if you don't keep to the terms of the contract?

If I say we're not finished, we're not finished!'

'Are you trying to blackmail me? What for? Anyway, it won't work.' Disbelief echoed in her voice. 'You can do what you damn well like; I'm not going back! I've finished the work I was paid to do, I'm boarding the plane in twenty minutes, and I'm returning to London whether you want me to or not! We're finished!'

She heard his deep breath and imagined the anger in his face. She didn't wait for his reaction. Hitting the disconnect button, she deactivated the mobile completely, and pushed the phone back into her bag. Pressing her lips together in anger, she rose impatiently from her seat as if propelled by some powerful force. She tried not to tremble. How dare he order her about?

Their working and personal relationship had ended. She ignored the voice telling her that it had been the best time of her life. Only someone with exaggerated self-importance and a distorted sense of power would try to force her to go back to the island! Who did he think he was, some kind of god?

She wandered uneasily up and down the departure lounge and wondered if it was true that she was breaking the contract. With his ruthless determination, it could mean the end of the agency if he sued them. He wouldn't be that odious, would he? Would he penalise the agency because he was angry with her? She suddenly realised he hadn't mentioned the necklace — in fact, he hadn't mentioned anything apart from his stupid book!

The boarding call came at last, and Rebecca marched determinedly to the queue forming. She only prayed that, even if his pride was hurt, he wouldn't destroy their agency. They'd never get a similar commission again if he spread the word. Thankfully, Jennifer was a great partner. She'd explain and they'd survive somehow. She'd put all her energy into finding new clientele.

14

When the plane landed, the weather matched her mood; it was grey and cloudy. Waiting for her baggage, she closed her eyes for a moment and felt utterly miserable. She'd walked into it with her eyes wide open, and only had herself to blame. Her usually lively eyes looked wearily out of the coach window on the way to the city. The future seemed pointless and dreary.

Her small bedsit felt cold and hostile after the warmth of Italy. After unpacking her case, she phoned her parents, and then Jennifer. Jennifer wasn't at home. She left a message on the answering machine to say that she'd be in the office tomorrow morning. Left with her own thoughts, and with no other distractions, she thought about the journey on his yacht, the time he'd kissed on the raft, or just the small moments of sheer happiness lately. His face haunted her. Whether he smiled, was thoughtful, serious or angry; the memories of him was her only lifebelt in a stormy sea. She reminded herself that he didn't trust her, and he'd never talked about their future together. It would have been wonderful to have a shared future. The last thought that flashed through her mind before she fell into a sleep of sheer exhaustion, was she'd never stop loving him.

Jennifer cradled a mug in her hands and listened with eyes like saucers as Rebecca explained. She occasionally uttered a word of encouragement, or dismay, and finally looked at her friend in amazement. 'You worked for him, fell for him, slept with him, and now you never want to see him again? I'm confused.'

'Jennifer! Do you realize we might be in trouble? What will happen to the agency if he channels his anger against it? I'm sorry!'

'The agency? Who cares about the

damned agency? We've survived worse than this. I'm more concerned about you.'

Rebecca avoided her friend's questioning eyes.

'Do you love this guy or not? That's what's important.'

It was a relief to say. 'Yes, I do, but it doesn't matter if he's my dream man or not, he doesn't love me. He suggested I stole his grandmother's necklace.'

'Hey! Correct me if I'm wrong, but he never actually said you stole it, did he?'

'Not in so many words, but he asked things like if I knew how the necklace got there. That's the same thing.'

'Is it? If he thought you were guilty, he'd have dragged you to the nearest police station. You assumed that he thought you were thieving, but I think you're climbing up the wrong tree.'

Rebecca shrugged her shoulders, pretending not to care. 'I wasn't high on his list of priorities. I was just a pleasant episode for a day or so; I helped ease his boredom.' Just admitting it to Jennifer hurt.

'From what you just said, you didn't just ease his boredom.' She giggled.

Rebecca blushed a pale pink. 'Who knows how often he's had similar affairs with other women before me?'

'Rebecca! Wake up! If he's a damned attractive man and wealthy into the bargain, and if he's as red-blooded as you make him out to be, do you honestly expect that he lived the life of a monk until you waltzed back into his life?'

'I couldn't live with someone I don't trust and who doesn't trust me. I'm not even sure if he was serious about me, or not. We never made future plans.'

Jennifer slapped the desk with the palm of her hand. 'That's what bothers me most of all, you bolted without talking it out.' She paused. 'Do you know what I think? You're frightened of getting hurt, and you ran away in case he was play-acting. That was daft. You should have found out where you stand.

It's better to face the truth, than to live with a 'what if' situation for the rest of your life.'

Rebecca fought her confused thoughts. 'Oh, what does it matter anymore? It's over, and I'm only worried now in case he sues the agency.'

The telephone rang in the adjoining office. Jennifer jumped up, spilling some coffee over her fingers. 'I'm expecting an important phone call; that might be it. Back in a minute!'

Rebecca bent her head over a pile of unopened letters. Most of it was junk mail, but it was too risky to throw everything away without checking. She was glad to concentrate on something else. The outer door opened and shut, and she heard voices in the small reception area where a part-timer dealt with initial enquiries and any visitors. She continued to slit the envelopes, didn't even look up at the sound of approaching feet.

'Morning, Rebecca! Hard at it, I see?'

She was completely gobsmacked by the sound of his voice. His overcoat was unbuttoned and revealed a dark-blue business suit and conservative tie. The clothes matched the classical lines of his face; the white of his shirt contrasted noticeably with the tan of his face. She caught her breath; and then snapped her lips together with visible haste. Her lashes swept down over her cheekbones.

She reached for another envelope. 'What — what are you doing here?'

'Unfinished business.'

She continued to sort through the papers without really registering them.

'You do that all the time.'

'What?'

'Shuffle papers, when you're caught off-guard.' He looked amused at her confusion before he sat down uninvited and relaxed into the chair. It creaked under his weight as he leaned forward.

She felt trapped and tried to bring her chaotic emotions under control. She forced herself to look at him. 'What unfinished business are you talking about?' She crossed her arms and stared determinedly. She couldn't think straight under his scrutiny.

'You, me, sex, San Andrea, the book, your stray dog, my work, your work, Grandma, the necklace, my telephone call. You name it! Whatever you like!'

Jennifer breezed into the room her mug of coffee still in her hand. 'Rebecca, I really think you should — ' She stopped mid-way when she saw Luca. 'Oh!'

Luca stood up, gave her a disarming smile and held out his hand. 'Jennifer, I presume? I'm Luca Barsetti. Rebecca has mentioned you often. Forgive the interruption, but I had to clear up some points with Rebecca. They couldn't wait.'

Putting her mug down, Jennifer shook his hand and waved generously in Rebecca's direction. 'Oh, by all means! We'll talk later, Rebecca. Nice to meet you, Mr Barsetti!'

He nodded. 'Luca, please!'

'Yes, okay, Luca!' She left.

Luca took off his coat, hung it on the coat-stand, and sat down again. He hitched up the leg of his trousers, and flicked at an invisible piece of fluff.

Rebecca followed Jennifer's departure with her eyes. Jennifer half-turned at the door. She looked at him and mouthed 'Wow'. Luca swivelled and waited patiently until Jennifer closed the door softly behind her. The dark eyebrows arched mischievously. 'So, where were we?'

Rebecca was mesmerised by those familiar dark eyes, and fought to control her swirling emotions. He didn't even need to touch her to set her whole body on fire. 'We weren't anywhere. You were.'

He rose and started to pace the small room. He reminded her of a caged panther, dark, sleek, beautiful, dangerous, and completely unpredictable. He wandered until he halted behind her desk. He rested his hands lightly on her shoulders. She was going to show him how unconcerned she was; that she was immune to his touch. A shiver began to form in her body and her lips trembled.

'Hmm! Let's see, where do I begin?

Here perhaps?' He bent right over her, his head and his breath fanned her face before his lips touched hers like a whisper, and shattered her defences.

Her eyelashes touched her cheeks briefly then she stared up into his face and willed herself to remain unresponsive. She kept her emotions under a semblance of control until his mouth swooped to capture hers yet again. Unwillingly, her mouth moved hungrily under his. With his powerful arms, he pulled her to her feet and spun her around.

He murmured in triumph. 'The perfect beginning to a perfect day. You bolted, but you still care for me, don't deny it!' His arms held her and he whispered into her hair. 'Why?'

Her body was melting against his, and it was pure pleasure. It was impossible not to want him. Her hands rested on his arms and she willed herself not to move, not to make the situation more unbearable. She licked her lip trying to remain sensible. 'Why do you think that I left? What — what about the necklace?'

He held her at arm's length for a few seconds and the dark eyes pierced her soul. 'The necklace?' Now he was staring absent-mindedly at her lips and his expression made Rebecca want to throw all hesitation to the wind. 'Oh, that! Antonia was behind it. She paid someone from the catering company to steal the necklace and the snuffbox when they cleared up after the party.'

Rebecca spluttered. 'She went that far?'

'Yes, her family are terribly shocked and embarrassed. Grandma won't press charges.'

'I almost feel sorry for her!'

'Do you?' His hands encircled her waist, and he stared knowingly into her face. 'Liar!'

An invisible web binding them together was busy tightening the knots again and it gave her a giddy sense of pleasure. It was almost impossible not to show how her happiness was growing inside. 'Well, I am sorry for your grandmother.'

He traced the shape of her lips with his finger, and Rebecca had difficulty concentrating. She had an aching need for him to kiss her again. She was shocked at how wanton she felt in his presence. 'You could give Gran a real lift, if you come back with me.'

Rebecca pulled away as far as he'd let her. 'Back where?'

'Italy, Taranto, San Andreas!'

A cold sheet of protest was beginning to cover her euphoria. 'Luca I thought you understood. I am not going back. My life is here. I have a share in a business; I have family and friends. The last thing I need is an affair with someone who wants to control me and spends his all private life in the limelight.'

He continued as if he hadn't heard; his voice was bantering. 'I wish you'd stop fighting me and admit we belong together. A couple of days on San Andrea, a trip around the islands on the yacht, a visit to my house, a meal with the family, perhaps?' He held her waist imprisoned with one arm, and turned one of her hands palm upwards with the other, to kiss the inside of her wrist. 'If I don't take you to see Gran soon she'll make my life a complete misery. She knows how I acted and thinks I don't deserve you.'

'Luca!' Disconcerted, she felt so confused and badgered she lost her voice.

He threw back his head and laughed. 'Oh, I wish I had a camera to capture your expression!' He released her suddenly and grew silent. His tone was decidedly more serious. 'Darling Rebecca! You still think I'm only after an affair, aren't you? Not long ago I told you that it had gone too far for that, and I meant it.'

Her heart skipped a beat, but she remained silent.

'I didn't realize that I was lonely until we met again a couple of weeks ago. Things that I used to enjoy doing before you came bore me to death now. Unless I know you're around, I don't feel alive any more. There's so much I want to show you, share with you. I want you to be the best part of my life, and I want to be a part of yours. I was shocked and desperate when Grandma told me you'd left. I never blamed you, and I'm sorry if you thought I did. I handled it all badly, but I thought you were so mad at me that I'd better get the mystery solved fast. I didn't reckon with you being so hurt, so mad and so defiant. Making the police find the real culprit was my way of pleasing you again. I wanted to come back with my apologies for anything that made you feel unhappy. I'd almost made that possible. Then Gran contacted me and told me you were leaving. My last chance was your mobile phone. I messed that up too, didn't I? My tactics of trying to intimidate you don't work, do they? You'll have to be patient with me, I have a rare talent of stepping on your toes sometimes — but if you give me a chance I'm going to prove how much you mean to me and that I'm putting you first in my life from now on. I'll be more considerate in future, promise! You know I never promise what I don't intend to keep.'

She could barely concentrate on his words when he was so close. She shook her head weakly in disbelief, but a dreamy look came into her eyes.

'Rebecca, I'm begging, and I never beg!'

She wanted to believe him, but didn't want to get hurt again. 'It won't work — we want different things from life.'

His eyes flashed with signs of impatience, and then he lifted them to heaven briefly. 'Lord, give me strength! What, for instance?'

'I don't want to lose my independence, so we're doomed from the start. I don't intend to spend my life being a social butterfly.'

'Who's asking you to be a social butterfly? You can do whatever you want to do as far as I'm concerned

— as long as I'm part of your life. I've never, never cared about any other woman in this way before, and I never will again. I'll do my damnedest to make our relationship work.' His eyes glowed with fervour. 'You know I don't give my word lightly.' He reached into the pocket of his jacket and took out a small box. The diamond flashed as he flipped the lid open. 'If you need some kind of proof, this is the best I can offer. I've never asked anyone to marry me before, never will again. I love you. I'm asking you, Rebecca Summer — will you? Will you marry me, and make me a happier and a better person?'

She stared at him, paralysed, before she said softly, 'You love me?'

He nodded and looked puzzled. 'Of course I love you! That's what this is all about.'

'You've never said so before!'

'Haven't I?' He looked surprised. 'Well, I'm saying so now, and promise to repeat that I love you till the day I die if you want me to.' He hesitated. 'You do love me?'

It took her a moment to react but there was a lazy seductive look to her expression as she held out her hand. He whooped, and slid the ring onto her finger before he swung her around, scattering the papers from the desk. 'Now it's too late. Never run from me again, Rebecca. If I act like an idiot, it's only because I love you — always remember that. I need to know you're there for me; life has no reason or rhyme without you.' His eyes sparkled. 'Well, can you get away for a couple of days, or not?'

Somewhere inside happiness was bubbling over. 'I haven't taken on any-thing new. I've only just got in.'

He nodded. 'Good. I'll organise our flight; you repack your bags.' He paused. 'On second thoughts, I ought to meet your parents too. Let's spend tonight here and fly tomorrow or the day after. We can celebrate tonight, just the two of us. If I can't make love to you soon, I won't be responsible for the consequences.'

She laughed and the blood coursed wildly through her veins. 'Sounds tempting.'

His hands took her face and held it gently, kissing her several times in quick succession. He was silent again as he studied her face. 'Why didn't you wait for me? Wait for me to explain? You must have known I'd come back to you.'

'No, I didn't! I wanted commitment, and was afraid you wanted less than that.'

'I thought women sensed when they had power over a man?'

'Well, this one didn't.' She threw her arms around his neck and kissed him. The kiss grew more passionate and they were both breathless when they drew apart. 'I love you, Luca, more that you can ever know. I think I've loved you since our university days.'

His smile widened and he said, 'I may have been blind to your attractions then, but I promise I never will be again.'

'Promises, promises!' She avoided his mouth. 'Luca! I want to go on working. You won't mind?'

'Not as long as you come home to me each night.'

Rebecca held him at arm's length. 'And children? You like children?'

He nodded. 'Of course! All Italians love children.'

'How many?'

'Three or four, or ten? What do you think?'

She laughed. 'Are you prepared to give up your work to look after them?'

He tipped his head to the side. 'Are you kidding? I will, if you manage to earn as much money in a year as I do . . . Otherwise, we'll find a solution that fits us both. Other couples manage, and they don't have the advantages we do. It's all a question of compromise and organisation.'

'Can I have that in writing?'

He threw back his head and laughed.

'If needs be! That and anything else you want.' He looked at her, smiling. 'I love you.'

'I'll have to learn Italian.'

He shrugged. 'English is so international these days. You don't have to. All the family speak English.'

'I'd like to for your sake. I love you more than you can imagine.' Suddenly emerging from the haze of bewildering happiness, another thought hit her. 'Hey! How did you get here? You were in Taranto yesterday.'

'Yes.' He looked a little smug.

'You flew!'

'First flight out this morning.'

'You flew? You got on a plane again?'

'I sweated blood and tears, but I had to see you, and flying was the fastest way. So you can tell just how much I love you. If you don't, I don't know how else to prove it. There's no one else on this earth I'd have done it for, except you.'

'That's absolutely wonderful.'

He nodded silently, absorbing with

contentment the look of adoration and pride in her eyes as she spoke. 'I don't know what I've done to deserve you.'

With a lopsided grin, he replied, 'Perhaps we deserve each other?' Gathering her into his arms, he held her snugly.'

She started laughing, and it quickly turned to tears of happiness as she studied his expression. They were both teetering on the edge of emotions that were hard to control; they were almost there at last — finding the haven in each other that they needed, and had failed to notice eight years ago.